All he wan...

Since the mom... n
in her hands, h...
mind off her. O. ... hands. A touch here, a
brush there, each one leading to wanting more.

It wasn't love. It was lust, pure and simple, and
he found fighting it exhausting. Every night
he battled the image his memory held of her,
keeping him awake long after decent people
slept.

Touching her was the same as sticking his hand
in a flame, and still he ached to touch her. No,
it wasn't love. But he couldn't deny it was the
closest he'd ever come to it.

Grabbing her hands, he pulled her to her feet.
As he looked into her startled eyes, saw her lips
parted in surprise, an electric bolt shot through
him. He'd have it over with, he thought—this
kiss he'd been dying for....

Dear Reader,

For some people, falling in love is the last thing on their mind, so it's a complete surprise when Mr. or Miss Right comes along. That's how it is for Dusty McPherson, the bachelor cowboy hero of—well, what else?—*Bachelor Cowboy!* But he isn't the only one *not* looking for love. Kate Clayborne has her life planned out, and falling in love—or getting married—isn't part of her future.

There's nothing quite as satisfying as watching two strong-willed people meet their match…and then tumble into love, no matter how many times they deny it or how much they fight it. Will Dusty and Kate give in and find their happily ever after? Do they really have a choice?

If this is your first visit to Desperation, Oklahoma, and the people who live there, welcome! If you're visiting again you'll find some familiar characters, and will have a chance to meet some new ones. I hope you love Dusty and Kate as much as I've loved learning and writing about them. And look for more Desperation romances in the future.

Happy reading!

Roxann

Bachelor Cowboy
ROXANN DELANEY

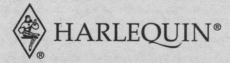

TORONTO • NEW YORK • LONDON
AMSTERDAM • PARIS • SYDNEY • HAMBURG
STOCKHOLM • ATHENS • TOKYO • MILAN • MADRID
PRAGUE • WARSAW • BUDAPEST • AUCKLAND

Recycling programs
for this product may
not exist in your area.

ISBN-13: 978-0-373-75296-6

BACHELOR COWBOY

ABOUT THE AUTHOR

Roxann Delaney doesn't remember a time when she wasn't reading or writing, and she always loved that touch of romance in both. A native Kansan, she's lived on a farm, in a small town and has returned to live in the city where she was born. Her four daughters and grandchildren keep her busy when she isn't writing, designing Web sites or planning her high school class reunions. The 1999 Maggie Award winner is excited about being a part of Harlequin American Romance and loves to hear from readers. Contact her at roxann@roxanndelaney.com or visit her Web site, www.roxanndelaney.com.

Books by Roxann Delaney

HARLEQUIN AMERICAN ROMANCE
1194—FAMILY BY DESIGN
1269—THE RODEO RIDER

Don't miss any of our special offers. Write to us at the following address for information on our newest releases.

Harlequin Reader Service
U.S.: 3010 Walden Ave., P.O. Box 1325, Buffalo, NY 14269
Canadian: P.O. Box 609, Fort Erie, Ont. L2A 5X3

To my grandchildren, Scarlett, Alexandria, Gavin, Jaxon and Becca, who help me see the world through the eyes of children and who are just beginning to understand that Nana is writing books while she sits at the computer all day.

Chapter One

"Keep your hands where I can see them, and back on down that ladder real slow." The voice was soft and low. Distinctly feminine. And definitely not joking.

Freezing at the command, one foot above the other on the metal steps of the combine ladder, Dusty McPherson stopped breathing.

An ominous click shattered the silence, and he knew without a doubt that the woman had a shotgun in her hands, cocked and ready. Breathing again, but careful not to startle her, he didn't question her as he eased back down the ladder. Beads of sweat broke out on his forehead, even though the late May Oklahoma morning sun hadn't begun to heat the day. A woman with a gun could be dangerous.

"Okay, that's good. Now turn around, but don't make any sudden moves," she said when he reached the ground. "And keep your hands up."

Dusty made his turn slow and smooth, his nerves taut and ready in case she had an itchy trigger finger. Knowing he could meet his maker in the blink of an eye, he faced his opponent. His eyes zeroed in on the tip of the steel barrel pointed directly at a spot any man would protect. He could only hope he'd be quick enough if there was any indication he'd be shot. He might want to be a daddy someday.

Slowly raising his gaze to her face, Dusty found himself staring into eyes the color of a clear blue mountain lake. It was all he could do to keep from sucking in air at the sight, but he managed to control himself.

The blue eyes widened for an instant, but just as quickly narrowed, hard as granite. "Just what do you think you're doing, cowboy?"

The urge to check out the rest of her was strong, but tempered by the fact that it could be the end of him if he did. Not wanting to spook her, he kept his voice low and even. "Put the gun down and I'll tell you."

"You must think I'm crazy." Her gaze never left his. She took a step closer. "What are you doing messing around my machine?"

"I'm here about the job," he answered with a calmness the clippity-clop of his heartbeat denied. "Agatha Clayborne hired me."

Her lips formed a perfect pink oval. "Oh…well…"

Dusty noticed her finger ease up on the trigger and allowed himself to relax a little. But he didn't let down his guard. Only a man with scrambled eggs for brains would do that.

Eyes narrowing again, she tightened her grip on the gun. "How do I know you're not just saying that?"

"You needed some harvest help, right?"

Her chin dipped a fraction of an inch in a noncommittal nod. "But I expected somebody younger. Like one of the kids from the high school."

"And I expected to get this wheat cut." He watched her consider his statement. "Mind if I put my hands down now?"

Hesitating, she finally lowered the shotgun. "Aunt Aggie mentioned she'd put some fliers around town. Maybe you should have come up to the house first and introduced yourself."

Before he could answer, she turned around, giving him a view of her backside and the long, copper braid that reached past her waist. The end of it swung between a set of slim but well-curved hips encased in a pair of tight blue jeans. Something about her was familiar, but he couldn't put a finger on what it was. And he was sure he wouldn't have forgotten the woman if he had met her before.

"You might as well come on in," she tossed over her shoulder. "Breakfast should be on the table."

Two strides brought him up next to her after he'd taken a long, breath-stealing look at the sashaying form in front of him. "Any special reason you came after me with that gun?" he asked, matching his longer gait to her shorter but strong one.

She slid him a look, but didn't slow her steps. "I don't like strangers poking around. Would you?"

"Guess not. But you didn't need the gun. I'm pretty harmless."

"You never know." She gave him another quick glance when they stepped up onto the wide porch of the Clayborne farmhouse and proceeded around to a side door.

She reached for the door handle, but he stuck his hand out to grab it at the same time. When his fingers brushed against hers she looked up quickly, a warning blaze in her eyes. He couldn't be sure if the sudden flash he felt was from the contact or the red light her eyes exhibited. He chose the latter and swallowed a chuckle. How was she to know she'd just issued him a challenge? Like waving a red flag at a bull. *Or blue, like those eyes.* With bulls, it didn't matter what color the flag was, as long as it moved. And she sure could move.

When they entered a sunny kitchen, the aromas of a country breakfast nearly knocked him over. His mouth watered at the tantalizing smell of sausage sizzling in a pan and hotcakes fresh from a griddle. He had traveled the rodeo circuit for more than ten years, living mostly on concession-stand food and tavern burgers, with an occasional restaurant and truck-stop meal thrown in. Home-cooked meals would be a taste of heaven.

Closing his eyes, he took a deep, reverent breath. It had been too long. Too damned long.

"Duane McPherson? I hardly recognize you. I haven't seen you since you were knee-high to a grasshopper."

Dusty opened his eyes at the sound of the strong female voice to find Agatha Clayborne studying him from head to toe, and he smiled at the quaint phrase from his childhood. It had been years since he had seen her. Well past her youth, her ginger-colored hair was peppered with gray. His gaze quickly settled on the heaping platter of scrambled eggs she held.

"Folks call me Dusty, Miss Clayborne."

"'Course they do. And I'm Aggie."

"I found him out looking over the combine," the redhead supplied from behind him.

Dusty felt Aggie's sharp blue gaze and heard her grunt of approval. "Well, you look fit enough to me."

"We expect an honest day's work," the redhead said.

His head snapped around at the words, and he looked back at her over his shoulder. Her eyes held skepticism, and he took offense to the statement and the inference. Never once in his life had he not given something his all. "You'll get it," he answered.

He slipped off his Resistol, noticing that when he did, Aggie's expression softened. She gave a decided nod and set the platter on the table. "Pull up a chair," she told him.

"You know how to drive a combine, don't you?" came the next question from the redhead.

Dusty gave the young woman a quick glance to let her know he'd heard her. She might be more than easy on the eyes, but she struck him as being one bossy woman. Just like his mother. He would rather deal with Aggie, who might have a bit of bossiness herself, but she had earned it. "I wouldn't be here if I didn't," he answered, focusing on the older woman. "I've handled machinery since I was a kid."

Again, Aggie nodded and looked past him toward the redhead. "He spent summers with his grandparents and then—" She turned her gaze on him. "You lived with them for a few years, too?"

"Four years," he answered. "All through high school in Desperation."

"They were good people. So was your mama. I was sorry to see her move to Tulsa after she married your daddy. Sorry they split up, too. How's she doing?"

"Good," Dusty said, although he didn't really know. He wasn't on good terms with his mother. Never had been. And his daddy had left when he was four.

"Families are a blessing, even when they're no longer with us."

He guessed she was referring to her brother. Tom Clayborne and his wife had been victims of an Oklahoma twister a year before the big tornado that hit Oklahoma City. It was obvious the redhead was Aggie's niece, and one of the two daughters they'd left behind.

And then he remembered where he had seen her. Only she hadn't looked like she did now. Not in high school. She was younger than him by three years and had been a new freshman his senior year. Yeah, he remembered her, although he didn't recall ever speaking to her. Back then, she was a lanky girl, all arms and legs, with a sprinkling of freckles across her nose and a haircut that would scare the britches off any guy. At the time, he'd had a girl, and he'd married her as soon as they both graduated. The marriage lasted all of six months. Like his father, rodeo and bull riding had called to him. And like his mother, that hadn't settled well with his new wife.

Movement across the room caused him to glance in that direction. In another doorway stood a blonde with a hesitant smile on her sweet face. The other Clayborne sister.

"I found the butter." Her anxious gaze bounced from the redhead to Aggie.

"Just put it on the table," Aggie said. She took a seat at the table and frowned at the others. "Now that we're all here, let's get to this breakfast."

Dusty stood, waiting, while the blonde took the chair directly opposite him and next to her aunt. He also noticed the diamond ring on her left hand, a clear sign she was taken, and he wasn't one to move in on another man's woman. Which left him the redhead. He couldn't decide if that was good or not, but he had plenty of time to find out. The summer he had thought might prove dull and wasted, while he waited out the time until he was released by his doctor to return to rodeo, might not be so boring after all.

KATE CLAYBORNE TOSSED her long braid over her shoulder and took her usual place at the table. Unfortunately, it was next to where their new hired hand was taking his.

He was no stranger to her. As soon as he had turned around on the combine ladder and she could see him clearly, she knew exactly who he was. But it was just as clear that he'd had no clue who she was. Not that she was surprised. Half the girls in the school had had a crush on him. Too bad she had been one of them.

The initial view of his backside hadn't been bad when she'd caught him on that ladder, either. She would have paid more attention, but she'd been too afraid he was a transient ready to steal the machine or strip the interior. One good look at him had been all she needed to recognize him, but she hadn't allowed her somersaulting stomach to overrule common sense and caution. Just because she knew him didn't mean she could trust him. And he obviously hadn't recognized her, even when his bourbon-colored gaze had met hers.

"Girls, this is Dusty McPherson." While she spoke, Aggie's attention was on the biscuit she was slathering with butter. Nodding in the direction of each of the girls, she introduced them. "These are my nieces. That one's Kate and this one's Trish."

Dusty looked up to smile at Trish. "This is great," he said, pointing at his plate with his fork.

"Oh, I didn't—"

"Kate did the cooking," Aggie said from across the table.

Kate felt Dusty's gaze on her, but pretended she didn't.

"You cooked this breakfast?" he asked.

Across from her, Kate saw Aggie's go-ahead nod, encouraging her. She knew what her aunt was thinking. It wasn't the first time she had tried her hand at matchmaking. But Kate wasn't interested.

"You'll find dinner filling, too," Aggie said, frowning at her. "We'll be cutting wheat in the field here at home to start, so we'll eat here at the house. When we get farther away, Trish brings it out to the field."

"And you're on your own for supper," Kate added to set the record straight.

"But I'll bring sandwiches in the evening," Trish chimed in. "We wouldn't want anyone wasting away." Her smile produced the twin set of dimples she was famous for, second only to her sweet disposition.

Dusty looked to Aggie. "Who's your truck driver?"

"I am," Kate answered sharply. What did he think she did, anyway, besides pointing shotguns at strangers?

His penetrating gaze fell on her again. "Any other talents? Other than cooking and firearms experience, I mean."

Ready with a hot retort, Kate looked up to see a spark of mischief in his eyes and knew better than to take the bait. Feeling his gaze slide over her, she lifted her chin to deny the warmth that went through her. "If worse comes to worst, I can drive a combine, change the oil, grease it and do minor repairs."

He rewarded her with a slow grin. "Multitalented."

"She really is," Trish agreed. "I wish I had her talents."

Dusty turned to her. "Each of us has our own."

"His or her own," Trish corrected and blushed fiercely.

"Trish is a teacher," Aggie explained. "Second grade. We all get corrected at one time or another. She's a writer, too. Just sold her first children's book."

Kate only half listened to the conversation around her, relieved that the subject had turned away from food. She loved cooking and baking, but it was a part of herself she didn't understand. She didn't know where her cooking flair came from. Her mother had been a good cook, but nothing spectacular, and Aunt Aggie was much the same. Somehow Kate had taken to it and added her own touch. She had even been providing pies and cakes to the local café and barbecued beef to the local tavern for the past few years. But it wasn't something she liked people making a big deal about. Farming was and always would be her first love.

Aggie pushed away from the table and stood. "When you're finished, Dusty, go on outside and I'll show you around."

If he had been anyone else, Kate would have offered to show him the farm and machinery, but because it was Dusty McPherson, she was glad she wouldn't have to. She had never reacted to any man the way she was reacting to him. Until she could get some control over that, being around him wasn't a good idea, but there wasn't much she could do about it until harvest was over.

Dusty laid his fork on the plate and rose from the table. "I can go out right now," he said, but his gaze lingered on the stack of biscuits.

"No need," Aggie said with a wave of her hand. "But Kate can add those biscuits to a basket. No reason why you can't enjoy them while driving the combine." She stepped into the hallway and turned around. "Kate, I need to speak with you."

Following her, Kate suspected her aunt had a few words to say about her rudeness. It wouldn't take more than a couple of minutes. Kate knew the routine well. She would apologize for being too outspoken and Aunt Aggie would forgive her.

Aggie waited until they were alone in the hall to speak. "I didn't want to say anything to Trish yet, as it doesn't affect her as much as it does you."

"What doesn't?"

Rubbing a fist across her forehead, Aggie hesitated for a moment before she met Kate's gaze. "I've decided to lease the farm after this harvest."

Kate couldn't believe what she'd heard. "You what?"

"I'm leasing the farm."

"No, you can't!"

"I have to, Kate. Fuel costs are up, and fertilizer, too. Repair on the machinery is costing a bundle, and getting a loan for new is out of the question. Even without those expenses, there aren't enough of us to do the work. With Trish getting married—"

"She doesn't have that much to do with the farming," Kate pointed out quickly, her heart hammering in her chest. The farm meant everything to her.

"Someday, you'll be doing the same."

Kate had no intention of getting married. "Then you don't know me as well as I thought you did," she said through lips stiffened by the panic she felt.

As if she hadn't heard her, Aggie continued. "I'm not getting any younger. I know we'd planned on you taking over the farm, once I retire, but you can't handle it on your own, Kate. Farming needs to be self-sufficient, otherwise it's nothing more than a hobby. And an expensive one, at that."

"We can find a way," Kate answered, determined not to let go of the farm. It had become her life.

Aggie laid a hand on her arm. "If the time comes when farming pays off again, you can end the lease."

"But—"

"No buts. I've made up my mind, as hard as it was to do. I don't mean to break your heart, but I don't want to lose the land, and that's what it could come to. You can understand that, can't you?"

Kate knew things had been getting worse over the past few years. After all, she did the bookkeeping. But she'd never dreamed her aunt would stop farming and lease the land to someone else. "If I can come up with a new financial plan for the farm, will you reconsider?"

Putting her arm around Kate, Aggie hugged her. "If you can do that, I will. It'd make that college diploma of yours worth its weight in gold. But I'll need to know at the end of next month."

Kate nodded, understanding that time was of the essence. Anybody leasing would want to start after the crop was harvested. But all it really meant was that she had little time to put together a plan.

Trish was the only one in the kitchen when Kate

returned, and she didn't look happy. "This is going to be a mess. I don't know how you're going to pull off the cooking and driving the truck. Aggie has always done the driving—"

"It won't be that hard." Kate gathered dishes from the table and scooted past her sister to the sink, her mind still numbed by her aunt's news. Not only had Aunt Aggie turned over the cooking to her long ago, but this year she'd had to give up driving the truck, too. If only Kate had paid attention, she might have seen the signs that her aunt might be thinking of retiring.

Starting the water, Kate added the dish soap before facing her sister and turning her mind away from her worries about the farm. "First off, this'll go much faster if you give me a hand with these dishes. I'll wash, you dry and put them away. And please put them where they belong, not just anywhere. I waste more time looking for stuff."

"But you can't cook dinner and drive the truck at the same time," Trish pointed out.

Kate gave her a withering look. "Of course I can. But if I have to waste time hunting for utensils, I won't get it done. And you know how Aunt Aggie prides herself on a smooth-running operation. Unless, of course, you'd rather listen to her rant and rave when dinner isn't ready on time."

Trish's usually sunny smile was turned down in a frown. She sighed, grabbing the silverware from the table. "I'll try to do it right."

"Good." Kate nodded and returned to the dishes. "I'll just have to come in after I've taken a full load of wheat to the elevator. It won't be a problem."

"I hope it works." Trish sounded unconvinced.

"It will." But Kate mentally crossed her fingers. She didn't mind doing double duty, but they'd all have to work together even more to make that happen. Time was of the essence during harvest. If it rained—and it usually did at some point—wheat cutting would come to a halt until the ground was dry again. A thunderstorm with hail could completely wipe out all of a small crop. She hated thunderstorms more than anything.

Trish reached into an upper cabinet to put away the plate she'd finished drying. "I wish I could drive."

"You have a license."

"I know, but it makes me nervous. And the thought of trying to drive that big old truck just scares me to death."

"It did me, too, the first few times," Kate admitted. "It's slow going, and takes a watchful eye to make sure someone isn't going to try to run you off the road because you're driving too slow. Can't drive too fast, either, or you could lose part of the load."

"Or turn the truck over in the ditch," Trish added. "I remember Aunt Aggie warning us when you first started driving it. She scared me to death."

Kate laughed at the memory. "Me, too, but that happening is pretty unlikely in these parts. I worry more about getting it stuck when rain moves in."

"Like that time when we went out to help at the south quarter and it started to rain. We nearly didn't make it home, and the truck was almost full. Aunt Aggie nearly slid off in that deep ditch."

"That was a nightmare," Kate said, "but we managed, just like we always do."

Hearing Aggie's and Dusty's voices outside, she hurried to the door, dripping water from her hands, and peeked out to see the pair moving across the yard to the combine. Walking back to the sink, worry started to nag at her. Maybe they wouldn't be able to do this. Scrubbing at a pot, she remembered that "maybe" was all she might have when it came to the farm. When her sister didn't say anything, Kate looked over her shoulder to see what she was doing.

Trish stood at the kitchen window, staring out at the farmyard beyond. "I wonder what he's doing back here in Desperation."

Kate turned back to the dishes and scrubbed furiously at the pot. "Why don't you ask him?"

"Why don't you?"

Kate shrugged one shoulder. "Maybe because it doesn't matter?"

"Sometimes I wonder about you, Kate."

Kate chose not to answer. Although only eleven months apart in age, she and her sister were like night and day. Trish had always dreamed of the day she would marry and have a family, while Kate had run away at the very thought of it. If she had her way, and she was determined to, she'd be like Aunt Aggie, working the land and enjoying life on her own terms. Not on someone else's. There'd be no compromising, no going places she didn't want to go, no making herself look pretty for someone who would never notice.

No, she didn't want a man complicating her life. But the real truth was that she had already lost two of the most important people in her life when she was fourteen. She knew, all too well, that someday she could lose her sister and aunt, too. Kate knew what she wanted, and it didn't include a husband—one more person she would love and possibly lose. She'd leave having a husband to Trish.

It didn't take long to get the dishes done and some leftovers gathered to take to Dusty. Grabbing the basket of food she'd prepared, Kate shoved her worry about Aunt Aggie's plans for the farm aside and hurried outside to the edge of the field where her aunt stood watching the new help get the combine ready for a long day's work. Dressed in blue jeans topped by a black T-shirt minus the sleeves, Dusty looked right at home on the farm, no different than any other hand from Texas to Canada. But on him, the jeans were snug enough to cause her heart to skip a beat. The faded denim fabric molded to his body displaying slim hips and long, strong legs. Broad shoulders topped a chest where any woman would love to rest her cheek—any woman but her. And his slim waist was encircled by a wide leather belt with a huge silver rodeo buckle that glinted in the sun. Sandy brown hair, a little too long and in need of a haircut, curled at the curve of his neck under the black Resistol that topped off his six-foot-something frame.

Oh, yes, he was something to behold. He always had been. And he was definitely aware of it and of his charm. She wasn't immune to him, but she had enough good sense to know it. Still, it was all she could do not to stare.

With a sigh of surrender, Kate hurried to reach them and set the basket on the hood of the big dump truck they would fill with wheat to take to the elevator. "Is everything okay?"

Dusty looked up from the combine engine, a grease gun in his hand and a grin on his face. He tipped his cowboy hat back with one slightly greasy finger. "This is a well-kept machine."

Kate felt a surge of pride. "My dad taught me to take care of things, and Aunt Aggie taught me how."

"You were a good student. You know what you're doing."

Kate's tongue stuck to the roof of her mouth, his sexy grin rendering her speechless. *Get a grip,* she told herself, dragging her gaze from his warm brown one.

Aggie walked up to place a hand on her shoulder. "Kate does everything well," she said with pride. "If it wasn't for her, this farm would have folded a long time ago. I was lucky when she and Trish came to live with me."

"We were the lucky ones." Kate turned to her aunt and smiled. "We couldn't have asked for a better home."

Aggie patted Kate's shoulder, her smile loving, but concerned. "We'd better get started. The day is getting away from us. We can get in a couple of extra hours of work with the wheat this dry."

Dusty finished the lubricating and wiped his hands on a rag. "Then let's get to it. There's a chance of rain in the forecast later in the week. This wheat is too good to let it sit."

Kate grabbed the basket of snacks from the top of the truck and handed it to him before he started up the combine ladder to the cab. "Here's something to hold you until lunch."

Taking the basket, his hand brushed hers, and their gazes met again. "Thanks, I appreciate it."

She froze, unable to speak or even nod. With every shred of determination she had, she dragged her gaze from his and turned for the house. "Don't let him get to you," she whispered to herself as she mounted the steps to the porch. "You have more important things to think about." Much more important than a rodeo cowboy with a melt-her-on-the-spot smile.

AFTER CHECKING the combine's controls and starting the engine to let it warm, Dusty took a peek in the basket Kate had given him. Finding it full of buttered biscuits, a jar of homemade jam and one of honey, his mouth watered again. He couldn't believe his luck. Not only had he found something to keep him busy until he could get back to bull riding, but he would be well-fed, too.

Glancing in the direction of the house, he couldn't ignore the seductively swinging hips of the sassy red-head. It was hard to believe she was the same shy girl he remembered from high school. He got the impression she didn't particularly like him, unlike other women, which presented him with a challenge. And a challenge always intrigued him. He wasn't planning on getting serious, just having a good time, since he couldn't do what he enjoyed the most. For the next few weeks, at least, which gave them plenty of time to get the wheat cut, he intended to get to know her a little better.

Setting the rotating reel on the front of the combine to the correct height needed, he put the machine in gear and watched the whirling cylinder sweep the shafts of wheat to where the grain-filled heads would be cut from the straw. He glanced back to see the bin behind the cab begin to fill with grain and felt a swell of contentment. He'd made the right decision when he'd called Aggie Clayborne about the job. Money wasn't a concern for him. He'd saved and invested most of his winnings, and his grandparents had left him their farm and house. But he had needed something to do. He wasn't accustomed to doing nothing.

Combining took only a part of his concentration. The rest of it he used trying to remember as much as he could about Kate Clayborne and planning the rodeos he would be entering, once his doctor gave the okay that he could. Work and thinking passed the time.

He stopped only to dump his full bins of wheat into the truck, watching as the golden, ripe kernels spilled out of the cylindrical auger and into the truck bed. Kate had been absent for most of the morning, except when she had appeared twice to drive the full truckload of wheat to the elevator and back again. But on this dump, he noticed Aggie behind the wheel of the truck. Climbing down from the combine cab, he took a half-hearted look at the belts and pulleys of the machine's innards, before he walked around to stand at the truck's door.

"Did my driver quit?" he asked, wondering what had become of the headstrong redhead.

Aggie stared straight ahead, her voice filled with vinegar. "Kate had some errands to take care of. I can drive this old truck."

Dusty tipped his hat back to get a good look at her and grinned. "'Course you can. Any reason why you don't do it full-time?"

She turned her head and looked him over, her eyebrows raised over snapping blue eyes. "Maybe because I don't like doing it?"

"If you say so." He didn't believe her excuse for a minute. Aggie had the same love of land and farming he sensed in her redheaded niece.

Aggie's stubborn expression turned to one of disgust. "Bad knee," she said in a low, embarrassed voice.

Dusty only nodded.

"I can drive some," she hurried on. "But I can't take a full day of it. Working the brake and the clutch is more than I can take after a while. If I do it for too long, I can't walk the next day, my knee gets to aching me so bad."

He could relate. His body had taken plenty of abuse riding bulls. "Understandable. I have my own aches and pains."

"Dinner should be ready by the time I get back from the elevator. Keep an eye out for Trish so you'll know when to quit."

He noticed the combine bin had nearly finished emptying, so he moved away. "I'm looking forward to it."

"Thought you might be." Aggie chuckled, but her mouth settled in a tight line when she started the truck.

He watched her drive away, bumping along the rough road, and then he climbed back into the combine cab to set the machine in motion again. Folks around Desperation admired the woman. She might be the brunt of jokes about her unmarried state, but Agatha Clayborne was a woman people respected. He was hard-pressed not to agree. And she'd raised a niece who had caught him off guard and had him wondering what the next few weeks might bring.

Chapter Two

The aroma of freshly fried chicken hit Dusty like a sledgehammer when he stepped onto the porch. He'd seen Trish waving to him from the edge of the field and had forced himself not to rush his last round.

Inside, Trish was crossing the room with a heaping bowl of buttery mashed potatoes in her hands. Having been raised a gentleman, Dusty hurried over to lend a hand.

"Let me help." He took the hot bowl from her and quickly dumped it on the table, wishing he'd thought to take the oven mitts, too.

Laughter rippled from behind him. "She keeps it warming in the oven until we're ready," he heard Kate say.

"I'll keep that in mind."

Kate took the same chair she'd had that morning. "Go ahead and clean up at the sink, and we'll get started. We don't wait on ceremony during harvest."

After washing and drying his hands, Dusty planted himself in the chair he'd sat in at breakfast, next to her. "Aggie should be back any minute unless there's a long line at the elevator."

"We can warm things up if there is," Trish said.

The platter of chicken Kate passed him drove any thought of work from his mind. He hadn't seen chicken so perfectly done since he was a kid.

Choosing a golden-brown thigh from the platter, he took a bite, and the chicken seemed to melt the instant he wrapped his mouth around it.

Before he could swallow and remark on it, the back door banged open, and Aggie entered, heading for the sink. "Those brakes feel kind of mushy to me," she announced, quickly washing her hands.

"I'll take a look at the brake fluid," Kate answered. "I need to remember to do the same with the old tractor. I noticed last fall that the brakes were kind of soft."

Dusty slid a glance at her, and his pulse picked up. But now wasn't the time, and he concentrated on the meal while the others discussed Trish's wedding plans and other womanly things that held no interest for him.

When he'd finished eating, the urge to kick back and enjoy the contentment of a more than satisfying meal was cut short by the need to get the work done. "I don't believe I've ever had better fried chicken," he said.

Beside him, Kate's chair scraped on the tile floor. "I'll get those brakes checked," she announced and jumped to her feet.

Dusty heard the door swing open and slam shut behind him. He looked from Aggie's pinched face to Trish's astounded one. "Did I say something wrong?" he asked.

"No," Aggie replied. "She just doesn't like people making a big to-do over her cooking or seeing the rest of us enjoying our meals too much when there's work to be done." She turned to Trish. "Let's get the table cleared before the heat settles in for the day."

Sensing he'd better get moving, Dusty grabbed his hat and strode to the door, eager to get back to work, too.

"Dusty," Aggie called when he pushed open the door. "See to it that Kate checks that brake fluid."

"Yes, ma'am." A backward glance at the plate Aggie was picking up told him Kate hadn't bothered to finish her dinner. While he was at it, he planned to find out what burr had gotten under her saddle and sent her scurrying.

He found her headfirst under the hood of the big truck, her feet off the ground, and the bottom half of her the only thing in view. And what a view! When he walked up behind her, his fingers itched to place themselves on her enticingly displayed backside, but he fought it.

He stopped less than a foot from her, still admiring her shapely bottom. "Need some help?"

Kate jerked upward and narrowly missed hitting her head on the hood. Sliding to the ground, she turned to face him, a belligerent tilt to her chin. "Do you make a habit of sneaking up on people?"

"No more than you did with that gun this morning," he reminded her. Her bright blue eyes sparked with green lights of fire under delicately arched brows. They stood staring at each other until his gaze dropped to a pair of lips so set in a frown, his only thought was to kiss them into a soft smile.

Slapping her hands on the same set of hips he'd been admiring from behind moments before, she snapped him out of his dream and growled. "What are you staring at?"

"Nothin'." He knew he had a grin on his face, but there was no way he could stop it. Not with the irresistible picture she made.

"Then let's get this wheat cut."

She turned to walk away, but he sidestepped and blocked her path. He pretended to look at the engine, crowding her, and caught the scent of spring rain, tempting him to take a deeper breath. Inhaling, he found he preferred it to even the aroma of the fried chicken they'd just finished and wondered what perfume she wore that could smell so good.

"Did you get that brake fluid in?" he managed to ask.

After hesitating, she moved away from him. "Of course I did. I know what I'm doing."

He turned slowly, gazing down into the deep blue pools of her eyes. When he spoke, his words were a husky whisper. "Do you?"

Kate opened her mouth, but immediately clamped it shut and spun on her heel. He watched her climb up on the bumper of the truck and struggle to reach for the hood. His gaze never leaving her lithe body, he moved next to her and pulled the hood down to within her reach. Without looking at him, she slammed it shut. He stood his ground while she walked around him and opened the door, nearly hitting him with it. Climbing into the truck, she gunned the engine.

"Let's get to it, McPherson," she said. She popped the clutch on the old truck and spun the tires, sending dirt spewing.

Watching her drive away, he shook his head. The more she tried to put distance between them, the more he wanted to close it. "Damn, this isn't going to be easy."

KATE STUCK HER HEAD in the living room and looked around. "Trish?" she called. "These sandwiches are ready."

When her sister didn't answer, she heaved an exasperated sigh and returned to the kitchen. "She's disappeared again," she told her aunt, setting the platter on the table.

Aunt Aggie sat at the table, one booted foot propped on another chair. "I'll bet she took off to do some writing. She was hunting for her notebook earlier while you were in here getting food ready. Or she left with Morgan, but I didn't see him drive up." Reaching over to the platter, she snatched a sandwich. "Any chips to go with this?"

Kate sighed again and reached behind her to pull a bag of potato chips from the cupboard. "Just a handful. Leave some for Dusty."

Aggie opened the bag and popped a chip in her mouth, a satisfied smile on her lips. "He's working out real good," she commented, reaching for another.

Kate grabbed the bag and pulled out a handful of chips, set them on the table in front of her aunt and folded the top of the bag over. "He'll do."

"You get along with him all right, don't you?"

Kate nodded. She couldn't tell her aunt how being around Dusty made her feel. She couldn't even explain it to herself. But she knew she didn't like feeling it, and she didn't like him telling her what to do. "Maybe you can take these sandwiches out to him," she suggested. She didn't want to spend any more time with him than she had to.

"Can't," Aggie told her, pointing at her elevated leg. "My knee's really been bothering me today."

Kate frowned. "I hope that doesn't mean rain." She

hated thunderstorms, and rain would put a stop to harvest for a day or two, at the least.

"Could mean a lot of things," Aggie replied.

Kate looked at her. "What's that supposed to mean?"

Aggie shrugged, picking up her sandwich. "Maybe it was just driving that truck today. Or maybe it's another sign that it's time I retired from active farming."

There it was again, and Kate wasn't sure how to answer. Was her aunt hoping for a different response from her than she'd had earlier, now that she'd had a little time to think it over? "You're not that old, Aunt Aggie. We both know that."

"Getting older every day," Aggie answered. "Now you get those sandwiches out to Dusty. I'm sure he's hungry again by now, and I can see the combine headed in this direction."

Kate looked out the door to the field. "He's hardly been out of it since dinner," she commented, more to herself than the other woman.

"He's a hard worker," Aggie agreed. "A good man, I'd say."

"A hard worker, for sure, but a good man? That remains to be seen." Kate turned back and noticed her aunt looking at her, a slight smile on her face. "Don't you be getting any ideas."

Aggie's eyes widened. "Who said I was?"

"Right," Kate said, unable to hide her sarcasm. Picking up the plate of sandwiches again, she stuck the bag of chips under her arm. "I guess I'd better get out there before he takes off on another round." Heading for the door, she grabbed a jug of iced tea.

"We've got a good week and a half of this if it doesn't

rain," she heard Aggie say as she stepped out the door. "Think you can hang on that long?"

"Sure," Kate answered. As long as she didn't have to spend all of it with Dusty.

The combine slowed and came to a stop as Kate reached the edge of the field where she'd left the diesel tank earlier before going in to fix the sandwiches. She waited as Dusty set the machine to idle and climbed down.

"I need to fuel up," he told her, eyeing the pile of sandwiches in her hand.

She handed him the plate and bag of chips and set the jug on the ground. "You go ahead and eat, and I'll fill the combine."

She had turned toward the tank when he grabbed her arm. "I can fill it," he told her, his eyes hard.

Pulling away, she tried to steady her suddenly thumping heart. "It's my job."

"Not by a long shot." He handed the food to her. "Do you think I don't know what my duties are as combine driver?" he asked, softening his voice with a smile. "And I won't waste away. Not after that dinner today."

Kate didn't move while Dusty put the diesel hose into the fuel opening of the combine, switched on the tank motor, and turned to her. "When you're the combine driver, you get to fuel it, okay?"

She wanted to tell him that it wasn't his decision, that as the owner's niece, she could decide who did what. But that meant engaging him in a conversation about things that really weren't his business.

When he'd finished refueling, Dusty accepted the sandwich she gave him and took a bite, looking as if he was lost in thought. "Aren't you going to eat?" he asked, motioning to the plate balanced on the truck hood.

Kate shook her head. "I'm not hungry."

"You didn't finish your dinner either," he pointed out. His gaze slid down her body and back up again. "And you sure don't need to be on a diet."

Kate's body did a slow burn, and she did her best to explain it away to herself as a flash of anger. But she knew that wasn't completely true. No matter how much she didn't want to be attracted to him, she was. But only a little.

"Clayborne women tend to be small," she said, wishing she could disappear.

"I've noticed."

Unable to vanish and needing to change the subject to anything else, she decided to try a topic that might hold his attention and keep him talking about himself. *Better him than me,* she thought. "I hear you were a champion bull rider."

His eyes narrowed. "I *am* a champion bull rider."

Kate shrugged, trying to shake off his intense gaze. "Sorry I got it wrong. Any reason why you're helping us, instead of riding bulls right now?"

"I'm recuperating from some injuries and waiting for a release from my doctor."

"What kind of injuries?" It wasn't that it mattered or that she cared. And it wasn't because she didn't want to return to the house. There was plenty of work waiting for her there, but she was curious and it would wait.

He gave her a sideways glance, and then stared off at something in the distance. "The usual. Ribs, shoulder, head. Nothing I haven't had before."

"And in the meantime you decided to cut wheat for the Clayborne ladies?"

"Whatever comes up," he said with a shrug of his broad shoulders.

"Then you weren't necessarily looking to help with harvest, just needed something to do. Don't you make plans?"

He turned to look at her. "Sure I have plans. I ride bulls."

"That's it?" She couldn't believe someone wouldn't have some kind of plan with a goal for the future. As with most professional athletes and especially one with the kinds of injuries bull riders dealt with, rodeo couldn't be all there was. "What do you do when you're not riding bulls? Off season?"

He studied her, his expression puzzled. "Why all the questions?"

Fearing he might think she had some special interest in him, she thought it best to back off a little. "I just wondered, that's all. Most people plan for the future."

"Some might."

"But you don't?"

His gaze was hard and determined. And stubborn. "My future is my present. Riding bulls."

"No plans for family? Retirement?" she asked, unable to stop herself.

Taking another sandwich, he looked back at her with a smile. "Retirement when it happens, but I don't expect it to be soon. Family never."

She had to bite down on her lip to keep from asking why family wasn't in his plans. She was pretty sure she knew the answer. When she was still in high school, she'd heard about his marriage and the subsequent end of it. She shouldn't have asked. It was really none of her business.

And he might just start asking her the same kind of questions. If she wasn't willing to discuss her own life, why should she expect him to share his?

She looked up to find him staring at her, and her breath caught deep in her chest. Hands trembling, she snatched a plastic bag out of her pocket and began stuffing it with sandwiches. Closing it, she handed it to him.

"I need to get this load taken," she said in a rush.

"What's your hurry?" he asked as she scrambled into the truck and started the engine.

She didn't miss the humor in his eyes and realized she was coming too darned close to making a fool of herself. As she drove the load of wheat to the grain elevator in Desperation, she scolded herself for her interest and for letting him see that he made any impression at all on her. She also reminded herself that he would only be around for a few weeks. After that, he would be gone, and life would be back to normal. Or as normal as it could be, while she searched for a plan to keep Aunt Aggie from leasing the land.

THE SOUND OF RAIN hitting the windows before the sun rose on Thursday morning put Dusty in a black mood. He had expected rain at some point, but the timing was bad. Just when he was enjoying his work, harvest would now come to a grinding halt for several days. He had always hated idle time and was usually either competing in a rodeo or on his way to the next one. During the few times there were neither, he accepted offers from friends to stay with them, and he always helped with chores or whatever was needed.

Not only would he miss the work at the Claybornes', but he would miss Kate. She had steered clear of him for the past two days, and he guessed it was because of her questions and his answers to them. He didn't often talk about his personal life, but she had been so straightforward, he hadn't been able to keep from answering. There was something so different about her that he was intrigued enough to find out just what it was that had him interested.

Standing by the old enamel kitchen sink in his grandparents' farmhouse, Dusty drank his coffee out of a chipped earthenware cup and debated what to do with his day. A glance around the room reminded him again that he needed to do some repairs and freshen up the place. He'd never used it and had given some thought over the past couple of years to renting it to someone. The farmland was leased to neighbors, and there had been nothing waiting for him here. No family, no children, no wife, only this house his grandparents had left him when they'd died six years ago. In that time, the place had aged, but a little bit of work would get it back into shape.

He finished his coffee, rinsed his cup and left it in the sink, then sprinted through the rain to his pickup truck to start the drive into Desperation for breakfast. With the weather good the first three days he had worked for Miss Aggie, they had accomplished a lot. Since returning to the area, he hadn't done a lot of socializing, and he was feeling the need for a little company. Somehow he knew at least one Clayborne wouldn't look kindly on him arriving at the farm when there wasn't any work to do. But the day wouldn't be a waste, he decided, ready to become a part of the community again, if only for a few weeks.

The drive was more like twenty minutes than the ten it normally took, thanks to the rain turning the dirt roads to mud, but it was worth the trouble. Once there, and with his fingers curled around a sweating glass of orange juice, Dusty felt the slight breeze from the ceiling fan stir the humid air in the small café. Eyes closed, he began to think about what it would take to fix up his house.

The metal clang of the ancient bell over the door broke through the noisy buzz of the room and claimed his attention, but he didn't move a muscle. The breakfast crowd had wandered in and out as he had ordered and eaten, leaving him to his musings, except for an occasional hello and a few rodeo questions from someone who recognized him.

"I need a man."

Dusty's eyes drifted open. Looking up, he saw a familiar figure posed just inside the door of the café, one fist propped on her denim-covered hip. The gray in her hair contradicted the strength and determination he recognized in her eyes.

The fan above him whirred as a hush fell over the room. His attention grabbed, he watched and waited, half curious, half amused to see Miss Aggie in action.

A burly man in overalls seated at the scarred counter swiveled around on a squeaky metal stool. "You've needed a man for years, Aggie. Don't you think that's a strange way to go about getting yourself one?"

Smothered laughter echoed in the background, but Aggie's narrowed gaze never wandered from the man. "Hmmph. A lot you know, Gerald Barnes."

Dusty swore the look she gave him would have shriveled most people, but Gerald chuckled and turned back to the plate of pancakes in front of him.

She sent a daring glare around the room before she continued. "I need a man to help bring in a load of pies."

Dusty shoved away from his table in the corner and got to his feet. "I'll help, Miss Aggie."

She turned to look at him, her eyes wide with surprise. "Morning, Dusty. I didn't expect to see you today. Thought you'd be taking it easy."

"I am," he answered with a smile, "but I'm more than happy to help you."

With a nod, she started for the door. "Pies are in the truck. Cherry, apple, peach and pecan," she announced and marched out the door.

Dusty's mouth watered at the thought of the pies waiting outside, even though he had just finished a decent breakfast. He could almost taste the sweet tartness of the pies, when a hand clamped onto his shoulder.

"I hear you're helping with harvest," Gerald said, stopping on his way to the door. "Don't let Miss Agatha get to you. She's a good one, no matter how much we tease her. And the meals alone at the Claybornes' are enough pay for a hard day's work. Just make sure you don't get on the wrong side of that redhead, or you could find yourself in Doc Priller's office with a case of ptomaine."

Dusty stared at the man, not sure what to say, until Gerald whacked him on the back. "Just kidding, son. You can't go wrong with Kate Clayborne's cooking. Enjoy it."

"I sure intend to," Dusty answered with a smile and followed him out the door.

After Gerald shouted a goodbye to Aggie, who waited at the back of the pickup parked diagonally at the curb, Dusty caught up with her. "Four boxes of them," she said, pulling off a plastic tarp in the bed of the truck. "Just be careful not to drop them."

"They're beauties," he said, peering into the boxes. "Three of each?" He reached in to lift a box, making sure he had a good grasp on the cardboard and didn't tilt it.

She took it from him. "There's more at home. Come on by later and have a slice. Or two."

Pulling out the second box, he grasped it in one arm. "Give me that one," he told her, nodding at the one she held. She settled the first in his other arm. "I wasn't sure if I'd be welcome at the farm, seeing there won't be any work done today."

"Won't be for a few more days, by the look of it," she answered, glancing at the cloudy sky overhead. "At least it's stopped raining for a while. We can't do with too much." She walked to the door of the café with a slight limp and pulled it open for him. "But there's no reason for you to be a stranger. We're always glad to have a little company, and I'm sure the girls are happy to spend some time with someone closer to their ages."

Dusty stood in the open doorway and turned his head to look at her, taking care to keep his voice low. "That knee bothering you, Miss Aggie?"

She started to shake her head, but shrugged her shoulders. "A little, what with this weather. But it'll get better. It always does, once the sun starts shining again. I expect we'll be back at work in a couple of days, if the weatherman was being honest and had a clue about the forecast. In the meantime, there's no reason why we can't enjoy the time off."

"That's what I'm hoping to do," he said, passing by her into the café.

After the second trip with the third and fourth boxes, Aggie thanked him for his help. Climbing into her truck, she settled in and rolled down her window. "I was serious about the pies at home."

"Thanks for the invitation, but I may take a rain check on it, depending on what I find to do."

Aggie squinted and looked up at the sky. "You might want to make that a sunshine check, but like I said, stop by anytime."

He watched as she backed onto the street and waved as she drove away. Yep, he was planning to enjoy the day, in spite of the weather. Kate had conspicuously avoided him after he had put a stop to her curiosity and questions, and Trish had been busy with other things. Aggie had been his only source of decent conversation, and that had been limited because they had been so busy.

Maybe, he thought with a smile, as he wandered back into the café, Kate would be done with her mad-on.

He'd hang around the café a little longer, before heading out to the Claybornes' for some pie. It wouldn't hurt to catch up on the latest town gossip—or even some more ancient—and he might pick up a few things about the family that employed him. He might even get a handle on Kate and what people thought of her. And if that didn't happen, he could simply enjoy the company. But he had to admit that it was Kate who was on his mind.

Chapter Three

"So this is where you hide out."

Startled, Kate looked up from her work to find Dusty leaning against the door frame of her tiny office in Desperation's old opera house. Her stomach gave a flutter, which she immediately ignored. "I'm not hiding out. I'm working."

Going back to her work and hoping that by ignoring him, he would take the hint that she wasn't interested, she was nonetheless completely aware that he hadn't gone away.

"Income tax preparation," he said, the sound of his voice nearer than before. "You're an accountant?"

Keeping her eyes on the paperwork in front of her, she pointed her pen over her shoulder. "With a diploma from the University of Oklahoma to prove it." Without meaning to, she looked up and directly into his eyes, but she held her ground. He would *not* charm her today. "Do you have a problem with that?"

"No, I find it interesting." He took the last few steps to her desk, and then perched on the edge of it. "Isn't tax season over?"

Kate felt her heart rate increase and frowned. She didn't like the feeling, and she certainly didn't like him being so close to her. "Usually, yes, but Tom Travers filed an extension back in March."

It was a good excuse and had worked well when Aunt Aggie had returned from making a delivery to the café that morning and told her that Dusty was stopping by the farm for a piece of pie. Not particularly pleased at the news and wanting to make some headway on a plan to keep her aunt from leasing the farm, Kate had decided her office would be a safe place. She'd been wrong.

And just why was he here? Not to have his taxes done, she was sure. "What are you doing here, Dusty?"

"I was at the café and heard there'd been renovations on the old opera house, so I came by to see and saw you in here."

He reached across the desk to her papers and pulled one toward him. "I never realized you were a number cruncher."

She quickly retrieved her notes and folded her arms on top of them. "Is there some reason you should know that?"

"Curiosity," he said with a shrug of his shoulders. "People are interesting. You can learn a lot just by watching."

When he leaned across the desk, she was too slow to react, and he managed to tuck a stray strand of hair behind her ear. Cursing herself for her racing heart and for not being on guard, she straightened her shoulders and leaned back in her chair. From that position, she figured he'd have to vault the desk to touch her.

"Yes," she said, then cleared the breathiness from her

throat, "people watching can be educational. Maybe you should go out and find more to watch."

"Take you for example," he went on, as if she hadn't spoken.

"Let's not."

"You're a hard worker," he continued, apparently oblivious to anything she said. "Dedicated to farming and, from what I've heard, more knowledgeable about it than many."

She looked up at him and wished she hadn't.

"Do I have that right?" he asked, his warm gaze on her.

Quickly looking at his shirt buttons to avoid that gaze, she shrugged. "If you say so. Now if you'll—"

"And now this." He pointed at the papers spread out on her desk, then turned his attention elsewhere. "The rain has stopped and the sun is out. It's a beautiful day out there, yet here you are, working away."

She didn't see any reason in trying to participate in the conversation, when he seemed to be the only one talking and certainly wasn't listening.

"What do you do for fun, Kate?"

The question took her by surprise, and she looked up. "Fun?"

"Yeah, fun. All work and no play make Kate a dull girl."

Feeling a bit insulted, she took a deep breath. "If I'm so dull, why are you still here?"

His mouth turned up in a slow, sexy smile. "Maybe I like the company."

She gave an unladylike snort. "And maybe *I* don't."

"Maybe we could go out sometime."

She couldn't believe he had said that. "Go out?"

"Yeah, like on a date."

"I don't date," she said, without missing a beat.

"You're already taken?"

"No, I just don't date." She didn't feel the need to tell him she had dated in the past. Those times were on her list of disappointments. She had always been too unsure of herself. From the moment she and Trish had arrived in Desperation, she had tried to stay in the background. And now it seemed Dusty was doing his best to pull her out in the open.

"Why don't you date?"

Her frustration at his digging was beginning to take its toll. Still, she reminded herself, she had dug into *his* personal life, asking questions she shouldn't have of someone she hardly knew. "I really don't have time for it. Besides, why do I need to date?"

For a moment, he merely looked at her. "That's the strangest question I've ever heard. I think mine was better."

"That's not a surprise."

"But I'll answer it anyway."

When he stopped to take a breath, she held up her hand. "That's okay," she hurried to say before he could get a start. "I retract the question."

"No, it's not okay. I want to answer it."

"There's no need to."

Again, their gazes locked, and he shrugged his shoulders. "If you say so."

She was relieved. She didn't need him or anyone else telling her how strange she was. She admitted it. But she hadn't been so different before the accident had taken her parents' lives. She and Trish had been like peas in a pod as children, happy and content, with more friends than they could count. The accident hadn't changed Trish much, but it had Kate. Angry and grief-stricken, she had taken scissors to her long red hair and whacked off the lengths that her mother had brushed every night. It had been a foolish, adolescent act, and she had paid the price in embarrassment later. Being different became her hallmark, and she was now accustomed to it, finally feeling right in her skin.

"I remember you in high school," he said, as if he could read her mind.

"I doubt that," she replied, knowing full well that she had stood out among others, at least for a while. Once Trish began making friends and her own hair had begun to grow out, Kate was able to disappear in the crowd of other students.

"I didn't say I knew you, but I do remember you, at least a little."

"Because of my hair," she said, accepting the fact.

"And you were new in the school. That's the way it is in small schools. I was new once, too, so I know what it's like."

She didn't want him to understand. She didn't want them to have anything at all in common. "Then you'll understand when I say that I have work to do."

"Checkmate. You win this game." He stood, but didn't move toward the door. "This doesn't let you off the hook though. I'm serious about you getting out more. I've traveled all over the country and beyond. Desperation is a great little town, but you can't really know how great until you have some perspective. The same is true in life." His sudden grin was devilish. "And dating."

She couldn't believe he was still thinking of that.

"You're equating extensive travel with dating? How do you come up with this?"

"The more people you get to know—through dating—the better your perspective, just like travel."

"Oh, really? Well, I'll keep that in mind the next time I plan a vacation," she said, knowing she really didn't care.

"In your case, I'd say you need to start small. Locally would do, and I'm more than happy to help with it." He turned and walked to the door, but before stepping out of the office, he turned back. "Looks like we'll be back in the field on Monday, if the skies stay clear. I'll see you then."

Kate could only stare. When he was gone, she breathed a sigh of relief. The tingles that always went off when he was around could go back to sleep. She was happy where she was, working the land and making extra money with her accounting business and a little cooking. She didn't need him or anyone else to provide entertainment. Or happiness.

WITH THE FIELDS still too wet to get into with a combine and the Saturday morning baking finished, Kate decided to take the rest of the day off and do nothing. Sitting at the kitchen table, flipping through one of Trish's bridal magazines, she heard voices and looked up to see her aunt limp into the kitchen on her bad knee, with Dusty right behind her.

"Pull up a chair and make yourself at home," Aggie told him with a wave of her hand in the direction of the chair near Kate.

Not wanting to be near him, after his appearance at her office two days before, and considering the effect he had on her, Kate jumped up. "I'll get that laundry finished."

But Aggie stopped her. "No, you keep Dusty company while I finish it."

"But your knee—"

"Gotta keep moving or it'll stiffen up more," Aggie said, as she disappeared into the hallway.

Knowing how bad-tempered her aunt could be when her knee was hurting, Kate did as she was told. Aunt Aggie's stubborn streak sometimes precluded common sense.

"I would think you'd be out getting more perspective on the world," Kate said, without looking at Dusty, as she returned to her chair and pretended to read the magazine.

He pulled out the chair next to her and sat. "A friend of mine's riding in a rodeo over in Altus."

"That's nice," she said, as unaffectedly as possible.

"I thought I'd see if you might want to go along."

She continued to flip through pages and prayed he couldn't hear how her heart had suddenly started thudding. "Sorry, but I have—"

"Dusty, would you like some pie?"

Kate looked up to see her aunt standing in the doorway and wondered how much she had overheard.

"That'd be great," he answered.

Aggie limped to the cabinet and opened it, pulling out a large plate. "What kind? Peach, apple, cherry or pecan?"

For a second, Dusty didn't speak, his brow furrowed in thought. "Peach. No, apple. No, make it peach."

Chuckling, Aggie placed the plate and a fork on the table. "Cut him a piece of each, Kate."

Kate again did as she was told and went to the counter, where she removed a dishtowel covering the four pies. After cutting a large piece of peach and apple, she turned to Dusty. "Are you sure you don't want to try the cherry and pecan, too?"

"Maybe later."

She hoped there wouldn't be a later. The sooner he left, the better. But if the gleam in his eye was any indication, later wasn't that far away. "Hand me the plate, would you?"

He jumped up to pass her the plate with a smile that made her breath catch, and then returned to his chair. "Now, back to my question."

"What question was that?" Aggie asked, taking her usual seat across the table.

"I answered it," Kate said, "or tried to." She shot a look at her aunt. Had Aunt Aggie been listening outside in the hall?

"I asked Kate if she'd like to go to a rodeo in Altus with me. You might know the friend who's riding. Shawn O'Brien."

"Of course we know him," Aggie said. "And all the O'Briens. I've known Tanner since he was born, and Kate and Trish both know his wife Jules. What event is Shawn competing in?"

"Bronc riding, like his uncle. I didn't know Tanner well until we met up, years ago, on the circuit. Shawn and I have team roped together some." Dusty turned to look at Kate. "So how about it?"

"I usually spend time with the family on Saturday," Kate began, "so I'm sure you understand—"

"No need to do that," Aggie said. Standing, she walked to the door and grabbed a set of keys hanging from a hook. "I thought I told you we planned to pay Hettie a visit. You know how much she loves your pies, and I haven't had a chance to see her for a while. Trish has been looking forward to it."

As if on cue, Trish stepped into the kitchen, her purse in her hand, and took one of the pies, before she hurried to the door with nothing more than a quick smile.

Kate glanced at Dusty, who held a forkful of pie on its way to his mouth, his smile reaching from ear to ear. She wasn't sure what to think. This was the first she knew about a visit to Hettie Lambert. "But—"

"Why don't you go on along to the rodeo with Dusty, Kate?" Aggie held the door open and Trish stepped outside. "We'll be gone most of the day. Trish wants to stop at the library before it closes. No need for you to stay here alone, when you can get out and enjoy yourself."

"No, I can't—" But her aunt was out the door, down the porch steps and almost trotting to the pickup, in spite of her bad knee, and Trish was already waiting at the truck.

Kate stood at the door and stared after them as they drove away. She couldn't imagine what Dusty might be thinking.

When she turned around, she saw that he had finished the first piece of pie and had started on the second. Setting his fork on the plate, he looked up at her, his grin challenging. "Afraid to spend time alone with me?"

She wasn't about to let him think that and offered a confident smile of her own. "Not on your life."

"Then let's go," he said, pushing away from the table and getting to his feet.

"I'm ready. Lead the way."

His gaze swept her from her head to her toes and back up again. "You're sure about that."

"Of course I am."

He glanced down. His grin sent her heart racing. And she realized what he was looking at.

She liked being comfortable when she baked and had slipped on her fuzzy purple slippers early that morning—the fuzzy purple slippers with the googly eyes.

Hot flames of embarrassment swept through her, and she knew her face must match her hair. "I'll get my boots," she squeaked and ran from the room.

DUSTY HAD TO KEEP from laughing out loud at the way Aggie had bamboozled Kate into going with him. He wondered if Kate had noticed and hoped she didn't. He had been sincere when he'd told her that she needed to get out more. And he was glad he'd had Aggie on his side to make sure she did. Now that he was getting to know her better, he was finding he was right about Kate. She was a knowledgeable companion, and he was enjoying spending time with her as much as he had suspected he would.

"How is it again that you know so much about rodeos?" he asked, midway through the bronc riding competition.

Beside him on the wooden bleacher seats, she shrugged. "My dad took me to a rodeo the first time when I was maybe three years old. I must have enjoyed it, because we went to more. I suppose I picked up the lingo along the way and probably asked a million questions."

Dusty would have been surprised to learn she *hadn't* asked questions. "You miss him, don't you?"

Kate stared straight ahead and pressed her lips tightly

together, then nodded. Dusty recognized her pain and turned his attention to the arena.

"There he is," Kate said, pointing to the rider in the chute. "There's Shawn."

Dusty looked across the arena and spied Tanner's nephew getting ready for his ride. "Yeah, that's him."

At the rider's command, the chute opened and the cowboy bounced out on the back of the bucking horse. Even for Dusty, the eight-second ride seemed to last an eternity, but Shawn stayed on until the buzzer.

"Not bad," Kate said.

"He could still use a little practice, especially with the spurring, but he'll get there. He definitely has what it takes."

"With a champion for an uncle, he has the support he needs."

Support, or the lack of it, was something Dusty knew a lot about. His mother had never supported his father's love of rodeo. In fact, her complaints about him never being home had driven him away. Dusty had been only four years old, but he remembered the fights, the slamming doors, and his father walking out the door. He had wanted to be just like his dad, and eventually he had followed in his footsteps, even down to a failed marriage for the same reasons. Dusty had thought his young wife had understood what rodeo would mean, but they were both too young and selfish. He bore her no grudge. It was as much his fault as hers. Hadn't he seen it happen with his parents? He wouldn't make that mistake again. In fact, he intended to be better than his father and had already proved he was, at least in the world of rodeo. His father hadn't ridden for years, and the last Dusty had heard, was selling used cars in Norman. That wasn't what Dusty had in mind for himself.

"Why don't I get us something to drink?" he said, turning to Kate, who was watching the excitement in the arena.

She leaned down and grabbed her bag. "I'll go with you."

He shook his head. "Just sit tight and enjoy."

"But—"

He didn't bother to explain why he needed to go alone. It was a man's responsibility to do those little things, and Kate might not understand that. In fact, he thought with a chuckle, she would insist that it wasn't.

While he waited in line at the concession stand, he could hear the announcement for the next rider over the loudspeaker, but he didn't recognize the name. It made him more eager to get the okay from his doctor so he could go back to competing. He wasn't one to stay long in one place.

Feeling impatient, he pulled his hat lower over his eyes to block out the sun. He was hot. He was tired. The air was thick with suffocating humidity. Except for that, he was enjoying the day. But he felt a headache coming on, something that had only started happening after the last concussion, and reminded himself to mention it when he saw his doctor.

"Hey, Dusty! You made it!"

He turned to see Tanner's nephew walking toward him. "Shawn, how's it going?"

The fifteen-year-old shrugged his shoulders. "Did you see my ride?"

Dusty recognized Shawn's disappointment in his

mediocre score. "It wasn't all that bad, Shawn. It takes more than a year or two of competing to get those higher scores. You know that."

Shawn's laugh lacked humor. "I scored an eighty-one on the first one, but that second bronc I drew was more than I could handle."

"It'll get better. Is Tanner here?" Dusty asked, looking around.

"Wyoming was getting cranky, so Tanner and Jules took him to the pickup as soon as my ride was over," Shawn explained. "I guess eight-month-old babies don't like all the heat and humidity. Jules has her hands full with the little guy, but she always manages to see me ride."

"I'm glad she was able to come to terms with rodeo and bronc riding," Dusty said. "It was touch and go there for a while with them."

"If it wasn't for her, I probably wouldn't be here."

"I doubt Tanner would have ever stopped you, but it's good you have her on your side, too. Tell him I'm sorry I missed him," Dusty said. "And Jules, too. And tell them to stop in and see me sometime."

"Any chance you might drop in and see *us?* I could sure use some roping practice or at least a few pointers."

"One of these days. Soon. I've been helping the Claybornes with harvest, but once that's done, I'll have some free time."

"Good. I'll pass the word along to the family." Shawn waved as he turned away and walked toward the parking lot, his equipment bag swaying against his leg.

Dusty ordered and paid for a soft drink for Kate and a beer for himself, and then he made his way back to his seat. "I hope this is okay," he said, settling beside Kate and handing her the soft drink.

"It's fine. I'm not picky."

"That's a surprise."

This time, she turned her head to stare at him. "You make me sound unreasonable. I assure you I'm not."

"No, just stubborn."

She swiveled in her seat to face him. "*I'm* stubborn? I'm not the one who—"

"Kate."

"What?"

"You *are* stubborn. But so am I."

Opening her mouth to reply, she quickly closed it. "At least you admit it," she said, adding a smile. "Did you talk to Shawn?"

He stared at her, wondering just what she had been doing while he was getting their refreshments. "Were you spying on me?"

Her blue eyes widened with pure innocence. "Heavens, no. But I know that after Shawn's ride is a good time to catch up with him."

"I talked to him. He was disappointed about his score, but I told him there wasn't any reason for that."

"He did have a good ride."

"Not according to him," Dusty said, chuckling. "But like I told him, he hasn't been competing all that long."

"Will the two of you be roping together again?"

"Maybe. It depends."

"On what?"

"On a lot of things. Will you come watch if we do?"

"It depends."

He nearly laughed at the way she had turned the

tables on him. Now that he'd gotten her away from the farm and her office, she was relaxed. Intelligence and beauty. What a combination!

"We need to do this again," he said, planning their next outing. She would never accept that this was a date.

She shook her head. "That's unlikely."

"Why?"

"This is a one-time thing, Dusty."

"You're not having a good time?"

"That's not the point."

He studied her for a moment and then said the first thing that popped into his mind. "Why does a beautiful woman like you hide herself away?"

She wouldn't look him in the eye. "I'm not beautiful," she said, turning away.

Taking her by her shoulders, he turned her back so she would have to look at him. "You're not? Could've fooled me."

For a split second, he thought she believed him, but then he felt her shoulders stiffen beneath his hands. "It's a good line, though," she said, even managing to smile. "You use it often, I'm sure."

He shook his head. "Only with beautiful women." But the head shake worsened the pain of his headache, and he didn't resist as she pulled away.

He was surprised when she touched his arm, concern evident in her eyes. "Are you okay?"

Nodding, he winced. "Headache."

"You should have told me," she said, taking his arm to tug him to his feet. "Let's go."

"It's all right, I—"

"Now. Do you want me to drive home?"

"No, I don't. I'm okay." But he gave in and followed her, knowing it wouldn't do any good to refuse. And he didn't really want to. He suspected his headache would only get worse the longer he was out in the sun. "You're one pushy woman. You know that, don't you?"

She stopped and spun around to face him. "No, I'm concerned. Maybe you simply don't recognize it when someone cares. But I'll be sure, from here on out, not to be."

With another spin around, she took off, and he had to hurry to keep up with her. She cared? He hated to admit it, but he almost liked her too much. She was all spit and fire. Not that he wanted to spend the rest of his life putting out fires. But for the time being, he was enjoying himself more than he ever had.

Chapter Four

Dusty lowered himself to the top step of his porch and let the sun warm him. With a long look around the yard, he went over his mental list of all the work needing to be done on the place. After the rodeo with Kate on Saturday, the fields had dried enough to get back to cutting wheat, and they'd been working hard in the fields with harvest all week since then. But it had rained again during the night, so if he had any notion of renting the house when he returned to the rodeo circuit, he needed to get started on the improvements as soon as possible.

Money wasn't a problem. He had enough in the bank from his rodeo winnings to build a new house, but he'd rather keep the one he had and fix it up. The house might be old, but it had a charm he wouldn't be able to duplicate and memories he wanted to keep. When the time came for him to retire, he'd have the house and the memories to come back to.

Ready and eager to get busy, he stood, and the steps beneath him creaked. He would start with them. He had ordered lumber and materials in Desperation and was expecting the delivery any day, so there was nothing keeping him from getting right to work. He'd get the old steps torn out and be ready when the new ones were delivered.

He gathered the tools he'd need from the shed and dumped them on the ground by the porch. As he pulled the crowbar from the pile, he heard the engine of a vehicle coming up the long drive leading up to his place.

He stared, not sure what to think about what he saw. The Claybornes' old pickup inched its way up the lane as if whoever was driving either wasn't sure they had the right place or wasn't sure they wanted to be there. When it stopped in front of the broken gate, he knew why. Kate was the hesitant driver. His heart picked up its thud-thud and he dropped the crowbar. He hated to admit it, but he'd missed her. After they'd gone to the rodeo, she'd done a good job of avoiding him.

"I wasn't sure you'd be home," she called out as she walked past the drooping gate and into the yard, "but Aunt Aggie wanted me to bring by your check."

He couldn't stop the grin that erupted at the sight of her. "It could have waited until Monday."

"She doesn't see it that way," she answered with a shrug, handing him a long envelope.

"Tell her thanks," he said, stuffing the envelope into his back pocket without looking at it. Sunlight hit her copper-colored hair and set it on fire, and the urge to reach out and touch it to see if it might burn him was tempting.

"Looks like you're busy," she said, looking down at the ground around him, avoiding even a glance in his direction. "I won't keep you."

As she turned to walk away, he found his voice. "I'm not that busy. Stay and keep me company."

She hesitated and turned to look at him. "I really ought to get back home. Aunt Aggie and Trish are off shopping with Hettie. No telling when they'll be back."

"So there's nobody there for you to talk to," he pointed out.

"I don't need somebody to talk to," she answered. "I like being by myself."

"Well, I don't," he admitted. *At least not until now.* Usually solitude was something he enjoyed at times. But now that she was there, he knew he'd be thinking about her the rest of the day if she left, and he wouldn't get much done. "How are you with a hammer and paintbrush?"

A smile turned up the corners of her mouth and her eyes glinted with mischief. "About as good as I am with shotguns and brake fluid."

"Good," he answered with a grin. "Can you make a decent sandwich? I know you can make a great breakfast and dinner with all the fixings, but there's not much here. I haven't stopped at the store since last week, but maybe we can come up with something. And to tell the truth, I'm about to starve."

Looking as if she was waging an inner battle, she finally shrugged her shoulders and smiled. "Aunt Aggie was one step ahead of you. She had me fix some lunch. It's in the truck. I'll get it."

His stomach grumbled in answer. "Let me help," he said, kicking a board out of the way.

"Don't bother," she answered. "I can get it. You just find a place to eat it."

"I heard I needed to watch for ptomaine if you

were mad at me," he called out, when she started for the old pickup.

She stopped and turned around slowly, flashing him a wicked grin. "I guess you'll have to take that risk. If you're hungry enough, that is."

Silently blessing Aggie for thinking of him, he chuckled as he watched Kate walk around to the passenger side of the pickup and couldn't help but notice how pretty she was. Turning back to his work, he pulled a board from the porch and wondered why some man hadn't grabbed her up and married her.

"You're going to have a real mess to clean up," she told him as she returned from the truck. Setting the old-fashioned wicker picnic basket on the porch, she looked around the yard. "Do you have a wheelbarrow?"

"In the shed," he answered, gesturing over his shoulder.

She headed in that direction and returned a minute later, pushing the wheelbarrow across the yard to where he continued to work.

"What's that for?"

"It's more efficient than tossing everything wherever," she answered. "Clearing away the debris as you go will take less work in the end. All you have to do is toss the boards and nails in here after you rip them off. No fuss, no muss."

When she leaned down to pick up a board that lay at her feet, he reached out and stopped her. "You'll get splinters."

She looked up at him, her eyes wide with surprise, and then at her wrist where he held her.

He quickly released her and stepped back. "Maybe we should eat first. I'll just go inside and clean up."

Stepping over the missing steps and onto the porch, he escaped into the house. In there, at least for a few minutes, he wouldn't be so tempted to do what his natural inclination kept urging him to.

KATE SILENTLY CURSED her aunt for sending her to Dusty's and especially for insisting on taking him some lunch. She loved her aunt to pieces, but it was plain that Aunt Aggie was doing a bit of matchmaking. Kate was sure it was because her aunt was hoping something— or someone—would take her mind off the news about leasing the farmland, but Kate didn't need or want to be distracted.

When she heard the door open, she looked up to see Dusty coming out of the house with an old green army blanket in his hands. Managing to avoid the missing steps, she moved to the porch and reached out to take the blanket from him.

"Kate," he said in a husky whisper as he moved closer. He was so close she could see a tiny white scar at the corner of his mouth.

"What?" she asked in a matching hoarse whisper. She watched, hypnotized, as he raised one hand and touched her face with his fingers.

"Ah, Kate," he said, sighing as he tucked a stray strand of hair from her braid behind her ear.

For one second, she thought he might try to kiss her, but he dropped his hand as if he'd suddenly come in contact with an electric fence wire and turned away from her. "Let's get this spread out," he suggested, his voice strained.

"Y-yes," she answered. "Let's do that."

Together they spread the blanket on the porch, neither of them speaking, and when they were done she edged toward the steps. "Maybe it would be better if I left," she said, and turned for the steps.

"No!" he shouted, startling her and bringing her to a halt. "No," he repeated, his tone softened. "I—" His sigh reached her, but she refused to look at him. "Look, I'm sorry. I didn't mean to—"

She slowly turned back to see him shake his head without finishing. She wasn't sure what was going on with him, but she knew she didn't want it to happen again. Maybe sharing lunch with him wasn't such a good idea.

"Come on," he said. "There's plenty of room for both of us. What did you pack for us to eat?"

As he picked up the basket from the porch Kate was still unsure if she should stay. But she knew that leaving would not only be rude, he might get the impression she was afraid of him. She wasn't. It was the feelings he stirred in her that made her want to run away.

Looking for a place far enough to keep some distance between them, her gaze landed on the railing at the far end of the porch. If Dusty would stay where he was and not move closer to her, she'd be safe.

Perching on the rail, she didn't know what to think when he suddenly rushed toward her, until she heard the sound of splintering wood. He grabbed her by the shoulders and jerked her into his arms, just as the wood railing fell away where she'd been sitting.

His laugh was shaky as he held her. "I should have warned you," he said, the warmth of his body pressed against hers making her light-headed.

So much for distance, she thought, pushing out of the

hold he had on her. "And I should have known better," she forced herself to say, her voice as shaky as she was feeling. "I've seen rotted wood before."

"There's plenty of it around this place." He sounded disgusted as he moved to pick up the basket where he'd dropped it and brought it over to where she stood. "The porch floor is safe. I crawled under it and checked. And you can lean back against the side of the house. It needs painting, but it won't cave in, I promise."

"I'll hold you to that promise." She bent to unpack the basket. "Help yourself. I hope it's okay."

She could tell he was surprised at the contents. His eyes widened and he grinned as she took containers of food out of the basket, and then he began to fill his plate with the meal she had put together for him.

"You made all this today?" he asked, looking from her to the last of the food she was unpacking.

Shaking her head, she pulled out a foil package of several slices of freshly baked bread. "Yes and no," she answered, unwrapping it. Handing him two thick slices, she glanced at him and saw his raised eyebrows. "Yes, I made it. No, not all of it today. Only the bread and the potato salad. The rest are leftovers."

"Not bad for leftovers."

"Get comfortable," she told him, reaching into the basket for the rest of the utensils and giving them to him. She was proud of her cooking, but it wasn't something she liked to talk about. She'd rather be praised for her farming skills than her cooking skills.

He sat on the porch, leaning back against the house and stretching his legs out while she set out the sandwich makings. She watched as he finished building his sandwich and took a bite.

"It isn't fancy," she told him.

"Doesn't need to be. It's unbelievable what home cooking can do to simple food," he said as he scooped more potato salad onto his plate. When his plate was full, he looked at her. "Where did you learn to cook like this?"

She shrugged as she began to fill her own plate. "Aunt Aggie I guess, but a lot of it came from old family cookbooks she kept. I added a few touches, here and there."

"That's all it took?"

His questions made her nervous, and she could feel him watching her. "I guess you could say that. Cooking isn't that difficult, and I do other things, too."

"Like greeting people with shotguns, maintaining machinery and driving a truck? Oh, and I forgot the accounting."

"Something like that." Uncomfortable talking about herself, she settled a few feet away from him on the edge of the blanket.

They fell silent as they focused on their meal, easing Kate's jitters. By the time she was nearly finished, she felt confident enough for conversation again and looked around. "I think it's great that you're working on this place."

"It probably needs more work done than I can do, but it's worth giving it a shot."

"What else needs done?" she asked. "Besides the porch steps and railing, that is."

"On the outside, a new coat of paint. On the inside,

probably paint there, too, and replacing the flooring and the cabinets in the kitchen."

"You can't live in it as it is?"

He brushed the crumbs from his hands and set his plate aside. "It's not that. I'm hoping to rent it when I leave."

The fork in her hand stopped midway to her mouth. "Leave?"

"You look surprised."

She shoved the bite of potato salad in her mouth and shook her head. Of course he wasn't staying. Why had she thought for even a second that he might be? And why should she care?

"The land is already leased," he went on. "Being empty as long as this house has been is the reason it's in the condition it is now."

For some reason, she'd lost her appetite. Picking up her plate, she stood. "Then you won't be returning to Desperation at all?"

"Now and then, maybe," he said with a shrug of his shoulders. "I told Shawn O'Brien I'd do some team roping with him when I could. I taught him to rope when he was a little guy. But that'll depend on what the doctor says. As soon as I get his okay, I'll be back to riding bulls, so I doubt I'll be back in Desperation again soon. And what are you doing?"

"I need to get home," she said, putting away the food and cleaning up the mess.

He shoved himself forward and started to help. "I thought you were going to stay and help me."

All she knew was that it was time to leave. She didn't know why. She didn't care. She just wanted to go home. "I never said I would. I have some things to do for Aunt

Aggie this afternoon." She saw the look of disappointment on his face and tried to ignore it. "Maybe some other time."

As she was closing the lid on the basket, he took hold of her hand. "Are you okay? You look a little pale."

It was the perfect excuse. "To be honest, I've felt better, but I'm sure I'll be fine, once I get home."

He released her when she looked up at him. "Something you ate?" he asked with a grin that put her even more off balance.

"Could be."

When she reached for the picnic basket, he tried to take it from her. "Let me get that."

"I can manage," she said, pulling it away from him.

"If you say so. But maybe I should drive you home."

"I'm fine!" She ducked her head and squeezed her eyes shut, ashamed at how she must have sounded. Taking a deep breath to calm herself, she tried for a smile. "Really, Dusty, I can manage. It's not like I'm really sick or anything, just not feeling my best."

The look of concern on his face made her wish she had kept quiet. What was wrong with her, anyway?

"Thanks for the lunch," he said as he walked with her to the truck.

"You're welcome. I'm glad you enjoyed it." She shoved the picnic basket into the cab of the pickup and climbed inside, while he stood at the open door.

"Drive carefully," he said, stepping back when she pulled the door shut and started the engine.

"I will."

She spent the short drive home telling herself that she wasn't disappointed that he would be leaving soon and that she was really glad he would be. She'd be much better off when he was no longer around, making her feel things she didn't want to feel. By the time she reached the farm, she still hadn't completely convinced herself.

ANOTHER LIGHT RAIN SHOWER during the night kept them out of the fields and fidgety for another day. Standing in the kitchen, wondering what to do while Trish was spending the day with her fiancé and Aunt Aggie rested, Kate heard a pickup as it rolled up the driveway. Even in the short time he'd been working for them, she recognized the sound of Dusty's truck, and she went to the door to see what had brought him to the farm.

"I thought I'd do a little work on my house today," he told her as he climbed from the vehicle and stood next to it.

She stayed in the doorway with the screen door open and nodded. She'd made a mistake the day before by appearing to care if he stayed or left, and she couldn't let that happen again.

"I could use some help," he said, not moving from beside the truck. "I finished tearing up the steps and knocking down the railing yesterday."

She wasn't sure how she should answer that. It wasn't that she didn't want to help, it was a matter of simply spending time with him when she didn't have a good grasp on her emotions. She wasn't accustomed to feeling that way. Unable to think of a reply, she turned and started to step into the house.

"I'm scraping paint," he called to her, stopping her. "Two would make it go much faster."

She looked back at him over her shoulder. "And what makes you think I would want to help?"

"I don't know," he admitted. He tipped his hat back with one finger and gave her a sheepish grin. "I just hoped you might. It's not much fun working alone."

Hesitating, she wasn't sure it was a good idea to go back to Dusty's. If she went, she would have to have better control of herself, and she wasn't completely convinced she could do that. He always seemed to take her by surprise.

"I'll even supply the food this time," he tempted.

She wavered and finally gave in. "Let me leave a note," she said.

Hastily scribbling her whereabouts on a scrap of paper in the kitchen, Kate decided her best bet would be to do a better job of keeping her distance from him and not allowing him to see a knee-jerk reaction from her about anything. She'd reacted foolishly, something she wasn't fond of doing, but had never been able to control. She sensed he had formed some strange sort of attraction for her, although she couldn't imagine why, unless it was because she was so different. In that case, she had nothing to worry about. He would soon find someone better. Maybe they could find a comfortable way to be friends and leave it at that.

Outside again, she found him waiting in his pickup. "Hop in," he told her as she crossed the yard.

"I'll drive myself."

"That's a waste of gas," he argued.

"Not from my point of view," she tossed back as she got in the old truck. Backing out, she noticed his frown, but dismissed it. Dusty liked having his own way. So did she. A good reason not to think there might be a chance they could get along for any length of time.

When she arrived again at Dusty's, he handed her a metal paint scraper. "I already have the back of the house done. The paint is coming off like snow on a hot tea kettle. It shouldn't take long." He led her over to the side of the house where unpainted wood contrasted with what had not been scraped. "Nice, long strokes," he told her, taking the hand she held the scraper in and guiding it slowly along the wood.

"I can do it," she snapped, and she instantly regretted it. But his nearness and the feel of his hand on hers unnerved her.

"Yeah, you probably can," he said as he stepped away from her.

Relieved to be able to breathe again, she steadied her hand and started in. They worked in silence for a while before she couldn't take the tension between them any longer. "Is the back ready to paint?"

"I started on it first, in case it was going to be a tough job. Didn't want anyone having to look at it until I could find the right method."

"Would you mind if I started painting back there?"

His hand stopped in midstroke as he turned to look at her. "You want to work in the back? By yourself?"

She nodded. "You'll be done here in no time. That'll give us a head start on the painting."

Laying the scraper down, he shrugged. "If that's what you want to do. I'll get the paint and a brush."

While Dusty went for the supplies, Kate spied a ladder resting on the ground against the side of the house. Dragging it to the back, she leaned it against the area ready to be painted and started up the rungs, testing it for stability with each step.

"Get down from there!" Dusty shouted from behind her.

She turned to look at him. "It's safe. Hand me the brush and can."

Setting them on the ground beside himself, he glared at her. "I said get down. You can do the lower half. I'll get the top later."

"That's ridiculous," she argued, holding firmly onto the ladder. She could imagine him trying to drag her down to the ground. "I've climbed a ladder before."

He stalked to the base of the ladder and grabbed her ankle. "You are one stubborn woman, aren't you? I don't want you up there when I'm on the other side and can't keep an eye on you."

"I'm not a child." She shook her foot, hoping to break his hold on her. "Let go."

"Not on your life," he said through gritted teeth. The stubborn set of his jaw eased, and he smiled slightly. "If you get hurt, Aggie will have to drive the truck. And you know how her knee is."

Kate rolled her eyes at him. Unfortunately, he had a point. She didn't expect to fall, no matter what he might think, but accidents did happen. By tomorrow they should be able to get back into the field and finish cutting the wheat there, and in another day or two, they'd be done for the year.

And any other year. But that was something she didn't need to think about.

Still, he was right. Aggie would have a fit if she had to drive the truck because Kate did something foolish like lose her footing or reach too far. "Oh, all right," she grumbled, climbing back down the ladder.

When she made it safely to the ground, he handed her the brush and paint can, and then reached for the ladder. "I'll just take this with me so you don't get tempted. You know where I am if you need anything."

Glaring at his retreating back, the ladder securely in his hands, Kate pried the lid off the can, stirred the paint with a clean stick and stuck the brush in, thankful, at least, that she didn't have to work near him anymore. She didn't mind the painting at all. In fact, she'd rather be doing it than scraping off the old paint. Seeing the smooth cream color spread over the wood gave her a feeling of satisfaction.

She'd been working for nearly an hour, without a word from Dusty, when she heard the sound of a vehicle coming up the long lane to the house, tires crunching in the gravel. Staying where she was, she continued to paint, but she couldn't help listening to find out who Dusty's visitor might be.

"What brings you over this way?" she heard Dusty ask.

She recognized Tanner O'Brien's deep voice when he answered. "I haven't heard from you for a while, and I wondered what you were up to."

"Just getting the place spruced up a bit," Dusty replied.

Feeling a touch of guilt for listening in on the conversation, she decided that as soon as she finished this last area, she'd stop and say hello to her neighbor.

"It's looking better than the last time I was here," Tanner said. "Except I'd get some steps put in, if I were you. That porch is a mighty big step up."

Dusty's laugh reached around the house. "They're on

order and supposed to be delivered in the next couple of days. I decided to go ahead and get this old paint off while I'm waiting."

"At least you're keeping busy."

"Come on inside and let me show you what I plan to do in there."

Their voices trailed off as they stepped into the house, and Kate couldn't hear what they were saying. Several minutes later, she heard Tanner's next statement clearly.

"I'm glad to see you're thinking about settling down, my friend."

"I'm getting the house ready to rent," Dusty replied.

"Oh," Tanner said, sounding a bit disappointed. "I guess there isn't much reason to ask if I could talk you into coming down to the ranch and giving Shawn some pointers, then."

"No reason why I can't. As soon as harvest is over, that is. It should be dry enough to get back into the field tomorrow," she heard Dusty say.

"How long do you think it will take?"

"Maybe a couple of days or so. Longer if it rains again though."

Kate's brushstrokes slowed. When she realized it, she began to paint more quickly.

"You know, he's itching to team rope again," Tanner was saying, "but there's nobody around that he wants to do it with except you."

Even from where she was standing, Kate could hear Dusty's sigh. "He'd better keep looking. Don't count on me. I can give him pointers on his roping, but I'll be busy bull riding."

Tanner didn't miss a beat. "You don't even know if the doctor will give the okay to ride again. Why don't you go get checked out?"

"I plan to. I've got an appointment—"

Kate let out a scream as the first of the blinding stings hit her hand. She opened her eyes to see several wasps circling in front of her face, and she screamed again as she stumbled and fell to the ground.

Chapter Five

Strong arms encircled her, and Kate felt a gentle touch press her wrist. "Wasps," she whispered through her clenched teeth. "I guess I wasn't paying attention and knocked against their nest."

"Tanner, there's ice in the freezer," she heard Dusty say calmly. "Would you get it?"

"Sure. Be right back."

Kate slowly opened her eyes to see her hand already swelling. "Aggie will kill me," she moaned, more from causing trouble for her aunt than the pain she was feeling.

"If the stings don't," Dusty muttered, examining her hand with a gentleness that surprised her. He looked up at her. "You aren't allergic, are you?"

Shaking her head, she closed her eyes to the pain. Her whole hand ached as tears started to fall.

"Don't cry, hon, we'll get you fixed up," he said, his voice soothing.

"I never cry!" But the tears fell anyway.

She felt the brush of his lips in her hair and thought of moving away, but she didn't have the control she thought she did. She knew she was in dangerous territory, but it felt so good being held and comforted against his broad chest. Just for a minute.

"It hurts," she whispered, letting herself go and crying harder. Sighing on a sob, she turned her head to the warmth of his chest, pressing her cheek to it. Just one moment to breathe in the scent, to feel the warmth of skin against her—

His skin!

Kate froze and opened her eyes. She could clearly see tanned, muscled skin, lightly dusted with golden brown hair, pressing against her cheek. She felt him slowly pull her away, and she dared to look up at him. His brown eyes had darkened as he gazed down at her, and his hand slipped up to cup the back of her head. She held her breath as his face neared hers, her eyes fluttering shut, as if they had a mind of their own. She wanted to say no, but the word wouldn't form on her lips.

"Here's the ice," she heard Tanner say, and she and Dusty jerked away from each other. "I found an ice bag and a bandage to hold it on and some aspirin in the medicine cabinet."

"Thanks," Dusty replied in a voice that sounded as if he was choking. "Let's move you out of this hot sun, Kate. Take it easy, though." He helped her up and led her around to the porch, gently sitting her down on the edge of it while he knelt in front of her. "It's going to hurt again."

Kate nodded. Tanner took her other hand and held it, while Dusty finished filling the ice bag from the tray of ice. "Squeeze as hard as you want to," he told her, giving her hand a comforting squeeze.

"Don't I need a shot of whiskey and a bullet to bite?" she asked.

Tanner chuckled beside her, and Dusty looked up at her, grinning. "A bottle of whiskey might work better. Maybe then I could have kept that muleheaded obstinacy of yours in check and you wouldn't have been around back by yourself."

"But I got a lot of painting done."

"And Aggie will probably have to drive tomorrow if this swelling doesn't go down," he reminded her.

She didn't bother to answer, knowing he was right. She could hope that by dinnertime tomorrow she would be able to get back to hauling. But first, she'd have to manage making breakfast and dinner, and that didn't seem very likely at the moment.

When he gently placed the ice bag on her hand, she winced, and he waited until she nodded to wrap the bandage around all of it. "You'd better keep it elevated tonight and tomorrow."

That would be impossible. With Aunt Aggie having to drive the truck and Trish still working on basic cooking, Kate knew she had to find a way to get through it all. She couldn't let her family down, especially when it came to the farming.

"It'll be better in the morning," she insisted, but noticed his eyes narrowing in anger. "I'll keep an eye on it, though," she added quickly.

"Sit right here and don't move," he ordered in a stern voice. "I'm going to clean up the paintbrush, and then if Tanner doesn't mind following, I'll take you home and he can bring your truck."

"I can drive."

By the look of his set mouth, Dusty's patience appeared to be wearing thin. "You will not drive. For once, do what I say and don't argue."

She could see the laughter in Tanner's eyes, but decided not to say a word. Dusty was on the edge of losing his temper, and she had a feeling if she pushed him on over, she wouldn't be at all happy with the outcome.

"Stay put," Dusty told her, and started for the side of the house where she'd been painting.

Tanner followed him. "Just the woman for you," he said as they rounded the corner of the house. "She'd make you a mighty fine wife."

"Not me. She's as stubborn as a bear after a hive full of honey," Dusty grumbled. "And more trouble than she's worth."

Kate gasped, surprised and hurt, and hoped no one heard her. She certainly didn't have any designs on Dusty and especially not on marriage to him or any other man. While it was true she was stubborn, he was just as much so, if not more, and he had even admitted it. If she could have gotten to her feet without her hand hurting, she would have gone after him and told him so, but she was feeling wobbly and light-headed. Staying where she was, she nursed her wounded pride.

When Dusty returned, she avoided looking at him, fearing she might give away her feelings—feelings she wasn't willing to admit to anyone, including herself. Once he was gone— She squeezed her eyes tight as he helped her from the porch. There were still a few days of harvest left, and she would get through it. After that, Dusty would be gone, and he could do whatever or go anywhere he wanted. She didn't care. Not after hearing what he really thought of her.

As he helped her to his truck, she decided then and there to make sure she never had to be alone with him again. The memory of the way he'd looked at her and the feel of his arms around her strengthened her resolve. Whatever had prompted his foolishness was no concern of hers, but she didn't want to give him the opportunity of doing anything like it again. Whatever these strange feelings she had for him were, they would fade away as soon as he was gone. She was certain of that.

"HARDHEADED, STUBBORN FEMALE," Dusty muttered. He drove with his foot to the floorboard after he had dropped Kate off at the farm and made sure Aggie was completely aware of the situation. Aggie had assured him she could take care of the truck driving and that Kate would be well looked after. She even tried to talk Kate into going into town to have the doctor look at the stings, but Kate had waved them all away, insisting she would be fine in the morning.

Beside him in the truck, Tanner laughed. "I've never met a woman more perfect for you, Dusty."

"You think that copper-haired spitfire is perfect for me? Then you don't know me very well. Kate as a wife?" He snorted and glanced at Tanner to see an odd look on his face. Not sure what it meant, he continued. "I'd have to be crazy to even think of it."

"You've had some mighty hard kicks to that head of yours," Tanner said, looking him over closely. "You're crazy if you don't try to rope and tie that redhead."

"Think again, my friend," Dusty replied as he turned into the lane leading to his house. But he had a hard time getting the picture of Kate's face, tears in her eyes as she'd looked up at him earlier, out of his mind. And the way she'd cuddled up to him had set him on fire.

Tanner cleared his throat. "Shawn is competing the week after next," he said, obviously changing the subject before the conversation went south. "If you get the chance, come on down and watch."

"I saw him in Altus last week, and he did a good job."

"Not quite good enough, if you ask him," Tanner said, chuckling. "And I think Jules would be happier if he'd stick to team roping or anything other than broncs, but she won't say it. Maybe you should give a little more thought to team roping with him again. He'd like to be able to enter more than one event."

"After being sidelined for the past six weeks, I'll be concentrating on the bull riding." But Dusty felt bad about not helping the boy he'd taught to team rope. "I'll stop in to lend a hand with the team roping, whenever I can, and I'll see if I can't find him another partner."

"What if you can't ride bulls anymore?"

Dusty took his eyes off the road to stare at his friend. "That won't happen."

"It could."

"No, it couldn't." Dusty wouldn't even allow the thought to enter his mind. Bull riding was his life, and he wouldn't even consider entertaining the idea that it would end anytime soon.

"What if you met someone?" Tanner asked.

"So we're back to that again, are we? Look, Tanner, I'm not the marrying kind," he answered. "I won't be trying the rodeo and wife thing again. Once was enough to learn my lesson."

"Jules and I seem to manage it well."

Dusty smiled at his friend's good luck. "You don't know how happy it makes me to know that. But there aren't many out there like Jules. She's one of a kind."

"That she is," Tanner agreed. "And now with the baby…"

Fighting the little bit of envy he felt, Dusty didn't hear the rest of what Tanner was saying. His best friend had not only found a dream of a wife and had a baby son, but he had won the National Bronc Riding Championship a few months earlier. Tanner's life seemed about as perfect as anything could get. But it wasn't the life Dusty had in mind.

"I know what I'm doing," he finally said, determined to live his life on his own terms.

"There are more important things in life than rodeo," Tanner said. "Especially as we get older."

Dusty understood what his friend was getting at, but Tanner's crazy notion about Kate was dead wrong. He wasn't interested in marrying her or anyone else. They could continue to be friends, until he was back traveling the circuit again, but beyond that, he didn't have any plans where she was concerned. And they *were* friends, even though it wasn't exactly what he'd had in mind the first time he'd laid eyes on her, but neither was anything serious.

"My mind is made up," he told Tanner, as he pulled up in front of his house and killed the engine. "I'm going back to riding bulls. Nothing is going to stop me. Not Kate Clayborne or any other woman."

In spite of his concern for her, Dusty didn't see Kate the next day. Aggie drove the truck without complaint, but he noticed at the end of the long day that she was limping even more than usual. He didn't even see Kate at dinner. Since Dusty was no longer working near the house, Trish had brought dinner and the evening sandwiches to the field. He hoped Kate's hand wasn't hurting her too much, but he wasn't sure what was worse, that or her avoiding him because she didn't want to see him. And he didn't know why.

The next day, Aggie again appeared to drive the first load of wheat to the elevator. Kate arrived to take the next load, and Dusty made it a point to leave the cab to ask about her hand.

"Are you sure you're okay to drive?" he asked at the truck window. "Is it still hurting?" He tried to take a look at it, but she kept it hidden.

She wouldn't even look him in the eye as she fidgeted with the truck's controls and started the engine. "I'm fine. Don't worry about it."

"I *am* worried about it," he admitted. "It happened at my house. How can I not worry?"

Kate turned to face him, a frown pulling at her mouth. "Afraid I might sue?"

"Sue?" he said, his throat closing to choke him at the thought. "No, it never crossed my mind. For crying out loud, it hasn't crossed yours, has it?"

"It might have." Shoving the truck into gear, she drove away.

But he'd noticed the look on her face and knew it had been the pain talking.

They finished cutting the last of the wheat late that

afternoon, and he never got a chance to talk to her again. Maybe it was a good thing, he decided. He had told Tanner that Kate wasn't the woman for him. No woman was. But he had a hard time not thinking about her.

With harvest over for the year and finding himself again at loose ends, Dusty spent the next day working diligently on his house. He worked until dark and was physically exhausted, but he felt good. His ribs didn't bother him, even during the most strenuous tasks, and he figured maybe he'd finally healed. The headaches came and went, with no rhyme or reason, and he did his best to ignore them.

Bone weary but invigorated by the progress he'd made, he fell into bed, planning what work he'd do on his house the next day. He tried not to think of how often he'd wished Kate had been there to help him. Every time he had passed the spot where she'd been stung, his heart had felt heavy. He tried not to think of her in those late, dark hours of the night. Lying in bed, his hands folded under his head, he concentrated on getting back on the rodeo circuit, competing in the bull riding competitions and maybe a little team roping with Shawn. But it wasn't long before his thoughts became more about bright blue eyes and a sprinkling of freckles splashed across a pert nose.

When sleep didn't come, he wondered if he needed something besides remodeling to keep him busy. He had hoped Aggie might ask him to help with the plowing and disking of the ground that would be needed to get the fields ready for fall planting, but she hadn't. He missed breakfasts and dinners at the Claybornes', not only the food, but the company as well. He missed Kate and wondered how she was getting along. Punching his pillow, he prayed for sleep and fought the images of her that drifted through his mind.

KATE WAS BUSY making pies and cakes for the upcoming bake sale before Desperation's annual box social. The swelling in her hand was gone, and baking gave her time to think. But there was one problem. She was thinking things she had no business thinking about.

When she heard the sound of a vehicle in the yard and then the knock on the kitchen door, she knew immediately who it was and ignored it. When the knocking continued and no one else answered it, she left the pie crust she was rolling out on the table and went to the stairs.

"Aunt Aggie, will you get the door please? Dusty's here, and I'm up to my armpits in pie dough."

"You'll have to get it, dear," Aggie called down. "I'm indisposed."

Kate couldn't imagine what her aunt would consider indisposed unless she was stark naked and dripping wet. With an exasperated mutter about the poor timing of some people, she hurried to wipe the sticky dough from her hands, hoping she could find a way to keep him out of the kitchen so she wouldn't have to spend time alone with him. She now knew what he really thought of her. Thankfully, getting no answer at the kitchen door, he was now knocking on the front door.

"You're looking better," he greeted her, when she opened the door. "How's your hand?"

"Fine. Is there something you need?" With all the things that had been going through her mind while she baked, Kate wasn't in the mood for a conversation with him.

"I was hoping to talk to Aggie," he explained.

"She's, uh, busy upstairs, but she should be down in a few minutes. You can wait in the living room," she told him.

He was staring at her, the intensity of his brown gaze unraveling her already thin nerves. "Aren't you going to keep me company?" he asked as she turned for the kitchen.

"I'm sure you can wait alone for a few minutes," she grumbled, walking out of the room. She didn't need his unnerving looks or time spent chitchatting about who knew what, and there was no telling how long Aunt Aggie would be "indisposed," whatever that meant.

If only her aunt would get a move on so she wouldn't be alone with him. Turning back to make sure he wasn't following her, she nearly ran into him. "Where do you think you're going?" she asked.

"I'll be more comfortable in the kitchen," he answered with a heart-tripping grin.

"Well, I won't," she said and continued on her way through the hallway.

With no way to stop him from following, she walked into the kitchen where the table was loaded with paraphernalia for pie baking.

He turned her around, brushing at her face with one finger, his touch featherlight, without even a glance at the table. "Did you know you have flour on your face?" he asked in a slow, lazy voice.

It took her a moment to start breathing again and actually form a reply. "As you can see, I'm baking pies and in case you didn't know, flour tends to get everywhere."

Aggie's voice rang out in the hallway, causing them both to jump back. "Did you say Dusty was here?"

"I'm in the kitchen with Kate," he called out, his gaze never leaving hers.

To Kate's relief, Aggie walked into the room. "Good, I need to talk to you before you leave, Dusty."

The look he gave Kate before turning to answer nearly melted Kate on the spot. "Ask away, Miss Aggie."

"Well, now," she began, a broad smile on her face as she looked from Dusty to Kate, "I meant to ask you before you ran off after harvest—"

"I didn't run off," he protested.

Aggie waved a dismissive hand. "Whatever. The thing is we could still use some help around here."

After a quick glance at Kate, he nodded. "That's one of the reasons I stopped by. I was going to ask you if you needed some help."

"We can do it ourselves," Kate said, jumping in to save her sanity. Weren't things bad enough already without him around every day again? He confused her. And she didn't like it. She didn't like the way he had her thinking of things she had never wanted.

Aggie sat at the table, pushing aside a pie pan containing the dough for one of the light, fluffy-crusted pies. "Kate is a little on the stubborn side, I'm afraid." She gave Dusty an apologetic smile, and Kate nearly groaned aloud. "She's had a difficult week, with the wasps and all, and pride keeps her from admitting she can't do it all."

"I'll be happy to help," he told her. "What is it you need done? Working ground?"

Aggie glanced at Kate, who shot her a pleading look. "Just getting the machinery ready—"

"Getting the machinery ready for working ground,"

Kate finished, not wanting Dusty to know anything about Aggie's plan to lease the land.

"I can do that," he said. "Will Kate be helping?"

Kate turned to face him. "Do you think I'd let you touch my machines without being there to make sure you were doing things right?"

"I wouldn't dream of it," he answered with a grin. "But I have a question for you." When Kate merely stood there looking at him, he continued. "How about taking a ride into Desperation for some ice cream?"

"Sounds like a great idea," Aggie said, before Kate could turn him down. "And take your time. I was planning to go into town to visit Hettie."

Kate stared at her aunt, wondering how she could get out of the corner she'd just been put in. "But what about the pies? There really isn't time for me to run off for ice cream."

Aggie waved a dismissive hand. "Plenty of time for the baking. I'll put what's left of the pie crust in the fridge and cover the rest. Everything will be here when you get back."

Kate searched for another excuse, but found none. Knowing she was beat, she shrugged her shoulders in defeat.

"Have a good time," Aggie called to them as Kate walked through the door Dusty held for her.

In his pickup, Kate sat ramrod straight, furious at having been railroaded into going with him, when she had been determined not to spend time alone with him. Aunt Aggie was treading on thin ice, and Kate wasn't going to let this pass without telling her so.

With a quick glance in Kate's direction, Dusty started

the engine and pulled out of the drive and onto the road. "I'm a Rocky Road fan, myself," he said.

"I only eat vanilla," she replied without enthusiasm.

"Vanilla's good," he agreed. "All those toppings to put on it. Can't beat an old-fashioned banana split."

"I only like chocolate on it."

He let out a whoosh of breath. "You sure are in a sour mood today. Scoot over here by me," he coaxed with a smile.

She wasn't falling for it. "We aren't on a date, Dusty."

"We're not?"

"No."

"I'll make a deal with you," he said. "You scoot over here by me, and I'll agree with you." He slid a look over her from the toes of her boots to the top of her head and waited.

She ignored her body's response. "Let's just get the ice cream."

They arrived in Desperation before she was forced to carry on any more conversation. For a weekday afternoon in the summer, the Sweet & Yummy Ice Cream Parlor, located a few doors down from her office in the recently renovated old opera house, was glaringly empty. She was relieved. There'd be nobody to see her with Dusty, no one to think something was going on between them. Far from it, if she had her way. She chose a booth in the corner, though, just in case.

"You're not very talkative today," Dusty said, as they ate their ice cream in silence.

"I have things on my mind."

"What things?"

She met his gaze, determined not to let down her

guard, no matter how hard he tried to get her to. With a smile she didn't feel, she said, "Nothing that has anything to do with you."

For a moment he said nothing and only stared at her. "Damn it, Kate, what's up with you? Would it help if I told you I've missed you since we finished harvest?"

She didn't want to hear that. He was making it more difficult to keep him at a distance. She had come to the point where she couldn't trust herself around him. Over and over she'd relived how he'd held her when she'd gotten stung by the wasps. How tender he had been when he'd put the ice bag on her hand and wrapped it. She'd told herself to forget it, but she hadn't been able to. And she hadn't been able to forget his comments about her to Tanner, either.

"I've been worried about your hand," he went on. When she didn't respond, he turned to stare out the window that looked out onto Main Street. "But I guess you're doing— Is that Vern and Esther?"

Kate looked out the window, too, to see a seventy-something woman chasing a man of similar age down the street. "You're surprised?"

"Well, yeah," he said, turning back to face her. "It's been how many years? And she's still chasing after him?"

Kate suddenly saw a correlation she could use. "Some people just don't know when to give up."

"Is that a challenge?" he asked, understanding clear in his bourbon-colored eyes.

She shook her head, dropped her spoon into her empty bowl and scooted to the edge of the booth. "Not at all. Just a statement about the way some things are." Standing, she smiled at him. "I think we're done here."

He tossed his paper napkin on the table. "Not hardly."

The ride back to the farm was blessedly silent. Kate was relieved when she finally stepped inside the kitchen, even though Dusty had followed her. She expected he would. He was a gentleman.

"Thank you for the ice cream, Dusty," she told him, aware that her aunt was watching them from her place at the table.

"I'm glad you enjoyed it, Kate," he answered, politely. But the look on his face said something else. She was relieved when he turned to Aggie. "When do you want to start on the machinery?"

"Let's wait until after the box social on Saturday," she answered. "Will we see you there?"

"I keep hearing talk about it, but I don't know what a box social is."

Aggie propped her foot on the chair. "Really? I would think you'd remember or at least know about them, considering how much you like to eat."

"So it involves food, huh?"

He listened intently while Aggie explained how it had begun in the oil rush days when the town was still in its infancy, and Kate looked on in morbid fascination. She already knew how the social would turn out. Morgan would bid on Trish's basket, and Morgan's uncle Ernie, who managed the retirement center and was a family friend, would be bidding on Aggie's basket. For the first time since her high school graduation, and at Aggie's insistence, Kate would have a basket of her own in the mix.

"How do the bidders know who the basket belongs to?" he asked.

"There are ways," Aggie said, glancing at Kate, who hadn't moved from the doorway leading into the hall.

Dusty looked at Kate before turning to grin at Aggie. "And the two of you aren't telling, are you?"

Kate didn't answer and neither did Aunt Aggie. As far as Kate was concerned, he could wonder, just like the rest of the men.

"Don't worry, ladies," he said, smiling at each of them, "you don't have to tell me anything. I'll be able to figure it out for myself."

When he turned to leave, Kate slipped out of the kitchen to try to sort through her feelings. She knew they needed his help. Whether they would be getting the machinery ready to sell or to get the fields ready for planting, it was as important as harvest had been. But she wished she and Aunt Aggie could handle it on their own.

From her spot in the hallway, she could hear him saying goodbye to Aunt Aggie, but she stayed out of sight.

"You drive carefully on the way home," Aunt Aggie replied. "We'll see you Saturday at the social."

Kate shuddered at the thought. She wasn't looking forward to it at all, especially if Dusty was going to be there.

THE NEXT DAY, Dusty drove to Oklahoma City to see his doctor. It was time to find out just how soon he could get back to rodeo. Aggie hadn't mentioned needing him to help with the ground work, just getting the machinery ready. But even if she had, he was hoping he might be competing again by then. All he needed was the doctor's okay to return to the life he knew and needed.

"The ribs and shoulder are fine, Dusty," the doctor told him after looking over the X rays. "They shouldn't cause you any trouble except maybe an occasional ache in bad weather."

"I can deal with that," Dusty replied, waiting for the rest of the diagnosis. "And my head?"

"The concussions," the doctor answered, nodding as he thumbed through a stack of papers in a file folder.

"I've been having some headaches," Dusty admitted.

"How bad are they?"

Dusty shrugged his shoulders, unable to look the man in the eye. Lying wouldn't help him, so he told him the truth, hoping it wouldn't bring bad news. "Most of them I can handle with some aspirin, but now and then, they're worse."

"That's expected with someone who has had as many head injuries as you have. As far as your daily living, I doubt they'll give you much more trouble than that. I'll give you a prescription for something a little stronger to take when they're bad enough that the aspirin doesn't work."

Dusty slowly let out some of the breath he'd been holding. "What about rodeo?"

Scribbling on a pad, the doctor glanced up at him. "What events are we talking about?"

Dusty cleared his throat. "Bull riding."

The doctor didn't answer right away. "That's a tough one. With your history of concussions, I strongly advise against it. The brain can only take so much trauma. It's not something you want to risk."

Dusty wasn't ready to accept that. "Just what are the dangers?"

Turning to give him a level look, the doctor removed his glasses. "I'll be honest with you, Dusty. Worst-case scenario, death. But there are others not quite so…final. There could be long-lasting problems with movement, learning or speaking. And there's always the chance of a subdural hemotoma, seizures, even stroke." He waited while Dusty digested the information. "None of those are anything you can ignore. I understand how important your riding is to you, but it isn't worth the risk of your health or your life."

Dusty didn't like the prognosis, but he also knew he was a professional, which gave him an edge. "What about team roping?"

The doctor seemed to be considering it. "Well, I don't see any reason why not. It's a lot different than bull riding. Just be sure you get loosened up first. But if you discover the headaches are getting worse, we'll talk again."

Dusty nodded. Bull riding was dangerous. There was no doubt about that. But he wasn't going to give it up. He was too good at what he did. And the doctor hadn't ordered that he couldn't.

On the drive home, Tanner called, and Dusty told him a little of what the doctor had said. "I'll spend the next couple of weeks helping the Claybornes and working with Shawn, if he's still interested, but after that, I'll get back to bull riding," he told his friend.

"Dusty—"

"It's my life, Tanner," he said quickly, recognizing the concerned tone in his friend's voice. "I can't quit. I don't know what I'd do without it."

"I can think of a couple of things."

Dusty wasn't in the mood to hear them. "Nothing is going to stop me from living my life."

"Unless you don't have a life to live."

Dusty ignored the comment, determined to show Tanner and the doctor and anyone else who needed showing that he'd be just fine on the back of a bull. He'd take one day at a time, the way he always did, and let worries take care of themselves. Except for one, he thought, after he'd ended the phone call. How was he going to find out which basket was Kate's at the box social?

Chapter Six

"We'll go to the library as soon as Kate finishes her lunch, Trish," Aunt Aggie said.

Sitting in the Chick-a-Lick Café with her family, Kate put her napkin on the table. "I'm all done," she announced and turned to Trish. "Is that our last stop today? I'd like to get home and get the last of the cakes baked for tomorrow."

"Who's baking cakes?" a deep voice from behind her asked.

Kate recognized the voice. Looking up, she saw Tanner and Jules O'Brien. "Stopping in for lunch?" she asked them.

Jules, holding baby Wyoming in her arms, sighed. "He's teething," she said, gazing at her son, "and neither of us have been sleeping well. We're hoping that getting him out and about will distract him. And, yes, I'm hungry."

"He's such an adorable baby," Trish said. "It's hard to think he would ever be grumpy."

"I know," Jules answered, with a tired smile, "and I love him to pieces, but some days, like today, I'm worn out. Luckily, Tanner's a patient man."

"Or so she thinks," Tanner said, slipping his arm around her and reaching over to tickle his son.

She smiled sweetly at him before turning to Trish again. "I haven't seen you to congratulate you on your upcoming children's book. I can't wait to read it to Wyoming."

Trish smiled. "Yes, it's exciting. Much different than teaching, although that's my first love."

"She's such a wonderful teacher," Kate said, "and now an author, too. I'm so proud of my big sister."

"The whole town is proud of her," Jules said. "And, Trish, don't let me forget to have you sign the copy I intend to buy as soon as it hits the bookstore."

"I'll be sure to remind you," Trish said, her cheeks taking on a pink glow. "But Kate has talents, too. I may be the writer in the family now, but Kate is the cook."

"Don't you mean Kate is the clumsy one?" Kate asked, feeling her own cheeks warm. "Evidenced by my run-in with the wasps."

"Dusty was pretty upset," Tanner told them all as Trish excused herself to speak to one of the other café customers.

Kate wished she had kept quiet about it. She had managed to deflect the cooking talk, but she didn't know how much Tanner had seen that day at Dusty's. She'd tried her best to put that part of the incident out of her mind, the same way she'd tried to put Dusty out of her mind, failing miserably at both.

"Tanner told me about that," Jules said and settled on the chair vacated by Trish. "Are you all right? It must have been awful."

"It was scary, but I'm fine."

Aggie stood and picked up her purse. "Kate, why don't you stay and visit with Tanner and Jules? Trish and I will go on to the library and you can meet us there later."

Jules looked up at Aggie. "We'll see you tomorrow at the box social, I'm sure." Then she leaned close to Kate and whispered, "Tanner and I want to talk to you about something."

Kate wondered what that might be. Although she'd known Tanner for years, she'd only met Jules a year before. They'd become friends, although not close friends, and she couldn't imagine what the two of them wanted to talk about.

When Trish and Aggie were gone, Jules turned to Kate, while Tanner strapped Wyoming into a high chair. "We're worried about Dusty."

Kate looked from Jules to Tanner. From their serious expressions, she could only think something terrible had happened. "Why?" she asked, afraid of what the answer might be.

Jules shook her head and glanced at her husband, who settled on the chair beside her. "This crazy idea he has of continuing to ride bulls when the doctor told him—"

"He saw the doctor?" Kate asked.

Tanner leaned forward. "He didn't mention he had an appointment?"

"I know he's been having some headaches and was waiting for the doctor's okay to ride again. And I did overhear him mention an appointment to you at his place the day I was stung, but other than that, no, he never told me."

Tanner looked down, avoiding eye contact. "He didn't exactly get the okay to ride bulls."

Kate knew what news like that would have done to Dusty. "What do you mean by 'exactly'?"

Shaking his head, Tanner still didn't look at her. "He's had too many concussions. If he goes back to riding bulls, there's no guarantee that he won't be permanently injured." He finally looked up at Kate and met her gaze. "Or worse."

Kate shook her head. "No, that can't be. He said he'd had some concussions, but—"

"More than a few," Jules said quickly. "He once said he was a pro at it."

Kate couldn't believe what she was hearing. She knew Dusty was stubborn, but to risk his life? "What can I do?" she asked.

"You might try talking some sense into him." Tanner's anger was only overshadowed by his caring.

"He might listen to you," Jules said, placing her hand on Kate's.

Kate couldn't imagine Dusty giving any weight to anything she said. "I doubt that." She looked at them and saw they didn't believe her. "But if you think it might help…"

Jules smiled, first at Kate, and then at Tanner. "I think he's finding some things a little more difficult than he ever thought they might be."

"He sure is," Tanner agreed with a smile and a glance at Kate. "And he can't see what's obvious to the rest of us."

Kate looked from one to the other. If they were thinking what she suspected they were, they were very wrong. Dusty was looking for only a little summer fun. And since she wasn't looking for anything at all, she'd gone along with it. Or at least that's what she tried to tell herself.

"He'll see it before long," Jules added. "Dusty's no fool."

"I don't know what either of you is talking about," Kate said quickly, "but I can tell you one thing. Dusty doesn't care a bit what I think, but that doesn't mean I won't try to talk some sense into him."

After Jules and Tanner thanked her and wished her luck, Kate walked to the library to meet Aggie and Trish, thinking about the news the O'Briens had given her. Dusty was the most stubborn man she had ever known, but in spite of it, she liked him. And she was determined to keep him from doing something that would hurt him, whether he liked it or not.

"I HAVEN'T SEEN Dusty, have you?"

Kate turned her attention from the bidding on Trish's basket at the box social to glance at her aunt. "No, I haven't either."

After her conversation with Jules and Tanner the day before, she wasn't sure she wanted him to show up. She still hadn't thought of a way to bring up the subject of his visit to the doctor.

Aggie looked worried. "I hope nothing has happened."

Kate hadn't mentioned anything to her aunt or her sister about what Jules and Tanner had told her, so there was no way they could know what was going on. She was also aware there was no guarantee that Dusty wasn't on the back of a bull at that very moment. All she could do was hope. "He's a big boy. He can take care of himself."

They continued to watch the bidding on Trish's basket as the amounts rose higher. The crowd that had gathered in the city park was enjoying it, laughing and shouting over each new bid, women teasing men about their appetites. As it always did, Trish's basket bore a pink polka-dot bow. Kate suspected Trish had told Morgan which one it was, and she didn't blame her. After all, the town's sheriff was Trish's fiancé.

But this year things were different. In addition to Kate having a basket, Trish had made all the food for her own basket, with no help from Kate or Aggie. She had done such a good job, Kate was busting with pride. Oh, there had been a few problems, like when Trish had wandered off and forgotten the chicken she was frying, but she quickly returned to take care of it after Kate found her and reminded her. There was hope for Trish's cooking skills yet.

Kate's contribution for the evening sat among the others waiting to be bid on, along with Aggie's. The only differences between Kate's sister's and aunt's baskets were Trish's pink bow and the blue bandana tied on Aggie's. Kate had always insisted that leaving out her own basket was to level the field, when the truth was she didn't want to spend the evening with some man who thought only of his stomach. But this year, Aggie had overruled. Kate's basket sported a blue gingham bow.

"Sounds like the bidding is over," Aggie said, "but I can't see who won it."

Kate stood on tiptoe and craned her neck to see through the crowd. "Looks like it was Morgan, as it should be."

In a matter of minutes, they could see Morgan claiming the supper, and then Trish and Desperation's sheriff made their way through the crowd toward them. Out of the corner of her eye, Kate saw Dusty walking their way from the street. He didn't look especially happy.

"I missed it, didn't I?" he asked when he reached them.

"If you mean Trish's basket, yes," Kate answered. "What kept you?"

He shook his head and chuckled. "Flat tire. Probably from one of those nails you insisted needed to go into the wheelbarrow. Too bad you didn't get to my place sooner that day. I might have made it here in time."

"If that's a compliment, I accept and thank you."

Aggie put her arm around her niece. "Kate's basket is coming up. You could bid on it."

Dusty turned to look at her, his brown eyes wide with surprise. "Oh, yeah?"

Kate shot her aunt a warning look. "There's no reason to do that," she told him. "After all, you wouldn't want to risk ptomaine."

He nodded, his expression solemn. "You're right. Which one is yours? So I know not to bid on it."

"What's this about ptomaine?" Aggie asked.

Beside her, Kate patted her arm. "It's an inside joke, Aunt Aggie. I didn't mean a thing by it and neither did Dusty."

"Kate's basket is just like mine," Trish said, joining them along with her fiancé. "The only difference is—"

"Trish fixed her own this year, without help from me or Aunt Aggie," Kate hurried to say before Trish could finish.

"And she did a fine job, too," Aggie added.

Trish wasn't to be outdone. "But Kate's basket—"

"It's all right, Trish," Kate said, noticing the mulish look on her sister's face and loving that she cared so much. "I doubt Dusty will want to bother."

"Oh, I don't know," Dusty told her, with a devilish

grin. "I've heard that ptomaine is treatable. And this *is* to raise money for benches on Main Street, right?"

"Absolutely," Aggie said, but thankfully didn't give Kate away. "You've met our sheriff, haven't you, Dusty?"

"No, I haven't had the pleasure." Dusty turned to the man and shook his hand. "Dusty McPherson. Glad to meet you, Sheriff."

"It's Morgan. Morgan Rule. Pleased to meet you, too, especially if you're *the* Dusty McPherson." He gave Dusty's hand a friendly pump before releasing it.

"If you're referring to bull riding, that would be me."

"Then it's a real pleasure."

"Thanks. And you're a lucky man," Dusty said, indicating Trish with a smile.

"I think I am," Morgan replied, putting his arm around Trish and pulling her closer. "I'm waiting to see if Kate's cooking lessons have paid off."

As the men talked, Kate was slightly surprised Dusty was getting along so well with her future brother-in-law. Morgan could sometimes be a hard man to get to know. Of course she knew Dusty was a gentleman beneath all that "Me Tarzan" attitude of his, but she was pleased he was so nice to the sheriff. She was even more surprised when he excused himself.

"I promised to spend time with some old friends, but I'll catch up with y'all later," he said with a wink at Aggie. "Nice to meet you, Sheriff."

After Trish and Morgan drifted away to share their basket, Aggie turned to Kate. "I guess it's just you and me."

Kate put her arm around her aunt. "That suits me just fine. Let them go off and enjoy their meal."

"Speaking of meals, isn't that your basket they're bidding on now?"

Kate turned around to look at the gazebo where Mike Stacy, one of the councilmen acting as auctioneer for the evening, was standing. "Is it? I can't—wait. I see it. It is mine."

"Then we'd better get closer. Once the bidding is over, you'll have to join the winning bidder for supper."

Kate hung back. Her stomach churned at the thought of being in the spotlight, almost as much as it did knowing she would have to spend the evening with a man who had no clue whose box supper he was bidding on. "Oh, please, Aunt Aggie, won't you do it for me?"

"Absolutely not." Her aunt took her arm and moved them through the crowd. "Who is that bidding?" she asked, when they'd moved toward the front of the crowd around the gazebo.

"I can't tell." But she knew it wasn't Dusty. In fact, after a quick look around, Kate couldn't see him anywhere. *Chicken,* she thought.

"Well, I'll be," Aggie said.

"What?" Kate asked, moving to get a better view.

"It's Gerald Barnes," her aunt told her, at the same moment Kate saw him. "I wonder what he's up to."

"Up to?" Kate asked. "He's probably just looking for a meal."

"Going once, going twice, sold to Gerald Barnes," the auctioneer shouted. "Now who's the little lady this basket belongs to?"

Gerald looked straight at her.

Feeling her face heat with embarrassment, Kate gave her aunt a pleading look. She did not want to do this.

Gerald Barnes? Why, he was Aunt Aggie's age, or close to it. Had he somehow discovered it was her basket?

"Get on up there, girl," Aggie said, giving her a motherly shove. "It's Kate's basket," she announced, and the crowd cheered.

But when Kate had made her way to the steps of the gazebo, Gerald was nowhere to be seen, and neither was her basket. Her embarrassment reached an all-time high.

Councilman Stacy leaned close to her. "He said to meet him over by the picnic tables. I guess he's feeling shy. But he must have wanted it pretty bad. His final bid was fifty dollars."

Shocked, Kate could only nod. It was more likely that he had taken the basket home to have all to himself. If he had, she wouldn't exactly be disappointed.

When she told her aunt, Aggie simply shrugged. "There's no telling with Gerald. He's an ornery cuss. Gives me more grief than anyone else, but he's a good, decent man. He wouldn't do anything to embarrass you. So you go on, and I'll catch up with you later. My basket is up soon, and Ernie and I promised to share it with Hettie."

The sun was setting and twilight was quickly settling on the town, making it difficult for Kate to see in the heavily shaded park. When she reached the scattering of picnic tables she looked around, but she didn't see Gerald.

Stood up. That's what she was. But if she was honest with herself, she was really relieved. The last thing she wanted to do was spend the evening with—

"Miss Clayborne?"

She turned and peered into the shadows in the direction of the voice. To her surprise, she saw Dusty walking toward her. "Where's Gerald?" she asked when he reached her and gently took her arm.

He led her to a spot under a tree where a blanket was spread. "He said he had something he had to do. I didn't want you to think he had just disappeared, so I offered to take his place."

"Aren't you afraid this might be your last supper?" she joked, but her hands trembled as she began to unpack the basket. This was much different than the picnic they'd had on his porch, and she was thankful that the setting sun and the low light would hide her nervousness.

He helped her and then leaned back against the rough trunk of the tree. "I have health insurance."

"Good thing." She handed him a plate.

"This sure looks good," he said, taking the fork she offered him.

"I hope you feel the same way after you've eaten it and are at Doc Priller's."

He laughed. "I guess I deserve that for teasing you." He was quiet for a moment. "It was nice of you to teach Trish how to cook."

The iced tea she was pouring from a thermos into a glass sloshed onto her hand. Bantering with him was easier than taking this whole situation seriously. She looked straight at him. "Why wouldn't I?"

"No reason. From what I've heard, Trish has always had your help."

"So?"

He shrugged and set his plate on his lap. "Not all sisters would do that. Sometimes there's jealousy between siblings."

"Not with Trish and me."

He patted the spot beside him. "Sit here. It's getting dark."

Not sure it was a good idea, but not knowing how to politely refuse him, she lowered herself to the ground where he'd indicated and reached for her plate. If nothing else, she wanted to keep things on a friendly but completely platonic level. This could be her chance to talk to him about his visit to the doctor.

When they'd been silent for some time and the park had settled into darkness, except for the soft glow of small lights scattered throughout the park, she felt the need to make conversation. "Fifty dollars is a lot to pay for an unknown meal by an unknown cook."

"Not really. It's no more than a meal in a fancy restaurant would be."

"But this isn't red snapper en papillote or a Greek salad with feta cheese," she pointed out. "It's homemade fried chicken, potato salad, applesauce—"

"And just as good as those other things, whatever they are. Probably even better." He set his plate aside and turned to study her. "How do you know about those fancy foods?"

"I've made them," she said with a shrug, "but they really aren't the fare for people in Desperation. Not on a daily basis, anyway."

"Have you ever thought of starting your own restaurant?"

"You're joking, right?"

"Why would I joke about something like that?"

"When would I find the time?" she asked. "With farming in the spring and summer and fall, and tax business in the winter, there wouldn't be much time for running a restaurant and especially cooking for it. Besides, I cook because I like doing it. Making a career of it would spoil that."

"It was just a thought."

Clearing her throat, she attempted to keep her voice matter-of-fact. "Gerald Barnes didn't pay for this meal, did he?"

She waited out the silence until he finally answered. "You guessed."

"It's pretty obvious," she said, laughing. And then she sobered. "But nobody knew the basket was mine."

"I did."

"But how?"

"Trade secret. I can't reveal my source. Besides, I wanted to do it. Trish's basket sold for forty dollars. Yours should be worth more."

"That depends on who's buying it." But she couldn't deny that it had made her feel special, even though being in the spotlight for only a few minutes had made her uncomfortable. It also gave her courage. She was ready to do what Tanner and Jules had asked of her. "You can't go back to bull riding, Dusty."

He sat straight up and stared at her. "What?"

"You can't put your life in danger."

For a minute he just glared at her. She obviously hadn't approached the subject in the best of ways, because if looks could kill…

"I can do anything I like with my life," he finally said and leaned back against the tree again, still watching her.

"But—"

"Can't we have a conversation without an argument?" His voice had risen in the dark. "Listen, Kate," he went on in a quieter tone, "what do you say we call a truce tonight? This food is too good to eat on an upset stomach. We might even find that we like each other."

Like him? She was beyond liking. Way beyond. But if that's what he wanted… After all, he had paid fifty dollars for a basket of food. "A truce it is then," she said, but felt like a traitor.

"Good." Picking up another piece of chicken, he took a bite and seemed quite pleased with himself. Or the chicken, she wasn't sure which.

"But I'm serious about the bull riding." The words came out before she could stop them.

"So am I," he replied without looking at her. "And that's the end of the subject. Forever."

Kate felt terrible. She had failed Tanner and Jules. She had failed herself. Worst of all, she had failed Dusty. And there was nothing she could do about it. The thought made her sick to her stomach.

"Would you mind dropping the basket off at the farm tomorrow?" she asked, getting to her feet.

"What? Why?" He watched her pick up her plate and put it in the basket. "Where are you going?"

"Home." For some reason the word stuck in her throat. "I'm sorry, but I guess I just can't go along with this truce, after all. What you're planning to do is wrong, and as a friend I can't let you do it. I'm sorry we couldn't finish our dinner, but—"

She left him staring after her. She could feel his gaze on her, until she knew she'd disappeared in the darkness. But she hadn't felt she had a choice. Dusty could be seriously and permanently injured while riding a bull. Or dead. Jules and Tanner had been wrong. Her opinion was of no importance to him. He would do as he pleased, no matter what the danger, and continuing to argue with him wouldn't change anything.

DUSTY WATCHED Kate walk away from him, until he could no longer see her. She'd taken him completely off guard with her question, and somewhere, deep inside, he was pleased that she cared. But he wasn't going to discuss his profession with her. He'd learned from his parents that it did no good. Besides, he'd be gone soon, and Kate would find something else to keep her busy. Or someone else, because a woman like her deserved someone. That thought didn't cheer him, but he'd be leaving in a couple of weeks, and he had hoped it would be with goodwill between them. He honestly liked her—probably more than he should.

After looking for Aggie and Trish at the park, but not finding them, he guessed they had all gone home. Feeling bad that he had been so harsh with Kate, he left the park and drove to the Claybornes' with the hope of smoothing things over with her. He parked his pickup in the drive, grabbed the picnic basket and approached the house. A star-studded night with a slim moon hanging high in the dark sky barely lit the farmyard, but he knew the way. Taking a deep breath as he mounted the porch steps, he welcomed the fresh country air. He'd check on Kate, leave the basket with her and then he'd go home.

Instead of going around to the side, he knocked at the front door. Lights burned softly inside the house where he could hear a radio playing an easy George Strait song. He waited, but when no one answered he knocked again, louder and longer, wondering what the ladies might be doing.

Not getting a response from his second attempt, he was disappointed. He had wanted some companionship for the evening. Someone to talk to, to share things with. But Kate had tread on a subject she had no right to broach and then left him at the park, feeling as if it was his fault. But with no one home and no way to talk to her, his only option was to go back to his own place.

As he started to turn for the steps and head home, he thought he heard a creak not far away. Stopping, he held perfectly still, straining to hear the sound again. Instead, he was rewarded with the startling noise of a squeaky sneeze coming from the far end of the long porch.

"Okay, who is it?" he asked in the shadowy darkness. But he didn't need to ask. Like ESP, he felt the presence of the woman who smelled like a fresh spring shower. "Come on out, Kate," he called to her. "You can't hide over there."

"Go on home, Dusty," she replied, her voice drifting from where he knew the porch swing hung. "Nobody's home."

He set the picnic basket down and walked toward the sound of her voice, his boot heels tapping on the wooden porch. He knew he should probably do exactly as she said, but her voice pulled him closer. "Why didn't you say something when I knocked? I know you saw me drive up."

"Did it occur to you I might not want company?"

He stopped in front of her, his eyes growing accustomed enough to the dark end of the porch to make out her form in the swing. "Are you feeling better?"

"I'm feeling fine, thank you, and I don't need company. If you knew me, you'd know that."

He detected a sad note in her voice. "I know you're a hard worker. You know more about machines than lots of men. You're smart—"

"Isn't that wonderful?" Her sarcasm stabbed at him. "What an enticing picture. Spread the word. Men will be lined up for miles just to get a glimpse of me."

She shifted in the swing, one bare foot tucked under her, the other dangling but not quite reaching the porch. Stepping closer, he nudged the swing with his leg, putting it in motion. "Feeling sorry for yourself?"

"Me?" She laughed, but it lacked humor. "Far from it. I decided long ago I'd rather spend my life like Aunt Aggie, never having to live under the domineering thumb of a know-it-all man."

Her words stung. "Is that what you think of me?"

"You're no different than the rest," she said with a sniff. "I know what you want, Dusty McPherson, and I know what can happen. The really sorry part is that you don't care."

He knew she was talking about the bull riding. The only person he had told what the doctor had said was Tanner, so he was sure that's where Kate had gotten her information. He'd deal with that later. But at that moment, all he wanted was Kate. The more she talked, the more he wanted to pull her into his arms and end the argument with a kiss. In the darkness, with the night cloaking them, his buried needs welled up to engulf him. Since the moment he'd met her with a shotgun in her hands, he hadn't been able to keep his mind off her. Or his hands. A touch here, a brush there, each one leading to wanting more.

It wasn't love. It was lust, pure and simple, and he found fighting it exhausting. Every night he battled the image his memory held of her, keeping him awake long after decent people slept as he tried to banish it and replace it with other things.

He couldn't conquer the nights when he was alone, and it was becoming more difficult each day in her presence. Touching her was the same as sticking his hand in a flame, and still, he ached to touch her. No, it wasn't love. But he couldn't deny it was the closest he'd ever come to it.

"I'll show you what I want," he growled, unable to fight anymore. Grabbing her hands, he pulled her to her feet. Looking into her startled eyes, her lips parted in surprise, an electric bolt shot through him. He'd have it over with, he thought—this kiss he'd been dying for since she'd caught him with her shotgun.

Knowing she wouldn't comply easily, he held her hands in his, moving them behind her as he wrapped his arms around her and pulled her closer. It was impossible to tell whose heart beat harder as he lowered his lips to hers. He felt her stiffen when they touched, ready to bolt. But he held her, gently brushing his lips across hers. His control slipped as he felt their softness.

"Dusty," she whispered, warning mixed with desire.

"Uh-uh," he murmured into her parted lips. Given the opportunity, he slipped the tip of his tongue between them, tasting the sweetness she unknowingly offered him. It surprised but delighted him when she responded with a moan, melting against him, the fight going out of her.

When he deepened the kiss she moved against him, and he gasped at his body's immediate response. And then without warning she twisted away, breaking free.

"This is wrong," she said. Her eyes blazed in the dark, and he couldn't be sure if it was from anger or passion.

"You enjoyed it as much as I did," he challenged her.

"I did not," she cried. She took a step back, setting the swing in motion.

He reached out to capture a wisp of hair loosened from her familiar braid. She tried to move away, but was stopped by the swing.

"Honey," he drawled, "you might be able to fool yourself by denying it, but that body of yours said it all without words." She flinched, but he couldn't stop. "The only question I have is what are we going to do about it?"

"Nothing." Her voice was husky, rough, but strong. "Absolutely nothing."

He stared at her, the sudden change in her chilling him, yet not enough to cool him to normal. "Maybe not," he said, without thinking. But the look in her eyes told him she was dead serious. "And maybe you're right."

"You know I am."

She pushed past him, nearly breaking into a run for the door. He watched, wishing he could stop her and take it back. He'd taken a step which might easily destroy both of them. Only retreating would end it, and maybe in time, repair it.

KATE STOOD INSIDE the house with her back pressed to the door, listening to Dusty's footsteps and the sound of him driving away. She could only breathe and blink as she touched her fingers to her kiss-swollen lips. What had gotten into her, letting him kiss her like that? *Wanting* him to kiss her like that? He'd told the truth, she thought with a shiver. She *had* liked it. She'd needed it. How would she ever convince him otherwise?

Chapter Seven

"Let's go, slug-a-bed," Aggie called from the doorway of Kate's bedroom. "Dusty will be here any minute."

Kate groaned, burying her head in the pillow. She had fallen into a fitful sleep just as the day had begun to lighten. Dusty was the last person on earth she wanted to face. "I can't."

"Are you all right?" The concern in her aunt's voice brought another groan. "What is it?" Aggie's voice drew closer. "Your head? Your stomach?"

My pride, Kate wanted to say, but she bit her lip and kept silent. Knowing she couldn't hide forever, she pulled down the sheet enough to uncover her face. "I didn't sleep well," she mumbled. "I'll be down in a minute."

Aggie moved from the doorway and stood next to the bed to place her hand on Kate's forehead. "You're pale, but no fever. Are you sure you're all right?"

"Just tired." Kate swung her feet to the floor and took a deep breath. "If you'll get the food out, I'll be down in a few minutes to cook it."

"I've already started breakfast," Aggie said, moving to the doorway. "Trish is stirring the scrambled eggs."

"Oh, no," Kate moaned. "They'll be burnt for sure."

"Probably," Aggie replied, laughing. "But you have to give her credit. She's really trying." The sound of a vehicle pulling into the drive could be heard outside, and she looked toward the window. "You'd better get moving."

Kate nodded, grabbing her clothes, and Aggie left her alone. Pulling her cotton nightshirt over her head, Kate thought about how Dusty tended to treat the mornings he worked as if he lived at the Clayborne farm, walking in the side door that led into the kitchen as if he was one of the family. If only Aggie hadn't taken a liking to him and hired him right off, life would be much simpler.

But Kate wasn't going to let her emotions or the sleepless night or anything else get the best of her. And that included Dusty.

After dressing quickly, Kate hurried to the kitchen. Trish was sent out to the yard, where Dusty and Aggie were looking over the machinery, to call them in to breakfast. By the time they came in the door, Kate had finished cooking and was in her chair, treating Dusty to her back. She wasn't yet ready to look him in the eye.

"Good morning, Kate."

She raised her hand in a wave and faked a yawn that turned into the real thing as he took the seat next to her. She wouldn't look at him, no matter what he said.

"Short night?" he asked.

She bit back a retort. Anything she said might be mistaken for the wrong thing, either by him or the other two.

"Kate isn't feeling well this morning," Aggie offered.

Kate squirmed in her chair. She didn't want Dusty to

think he'd had any earth-shattering effect on her, although that's exactly what had happened. "I think it was something I ate last night," she said. "Or maybe the company?"

After flashing him a brilliant smile, without really looking at him, she turned her attention to her breakfast. But she couldn't ignore Aunt Aggie's questioning looks. Her aunt sometimes had radar that zoned in on her feelings, so she needed to tread carefully.

And Dusty's expression was priceless, when she sneaked a look at him.

"I'll be back to help clean up," Kate said, evacuating her chair long before the rest had finished eating. "I have some chores to get done this morning." An outright lie, it worked anyway.

Escaping to her room to avoid the possibility of having to actually talk to Dusty, she thought about her options. With him at the farm helping get the machinery in top shape, there wasn't any way she could continue to avoid him. And staying on her toes constantly would quickly become impossible. Just look what had happened last night!

She was making her bed after straightening the room when Aggie appeared in the doorway. "I want to talk to you, miss."

Kate glanced up with what she hoped was an innocent smile. "Is breakfast over?"

"I'll be downstairs," Aggie announced without answering and left as quietly as she'd arrived, closing the door behind her.

With a sigh, Kate knew she was in for a lecture. She'd been on the brink of rude, and one thing her parents and Aunt Aggie had drilled into both the girls was civility. Kate certainly hadn't exhibited any of that to Dusty at breakfast.

Knowing that if she took too much time her aunt would be back, demanding to know what was taking so long, she finished and went downstairs. She found Aunt Aggie at the kitchen table, a cup of coffee in her hands.

"Blame my rudeness on lack of sleep," Kate attempted before the tongue-lashing she knew was coming would hit.

"That's not it," Aggie said, studying her. Her lips a thin line, her aunt's gaze didn't falter. "Sit down," she said with a curt nod.

"I'd rather stand." Kate nearly quaked at the silence that followed.

Aggie shrugged her shoulders. "Suit yourself. But I have one question."

"What's that?"

"What's gotten into you?"

"I don't understand what you mean," Kate answered. And she didn't. Except for this morning, she'd been going about her life as she always had. Or trying to.

"You need a man, Kate," Aggie insisted, "as much if not more than Trish. I don't know why you can't see that and see that Dusty is interested."

Frightened they might be overheard, Kate turned to look out the door. Dusty might be able to hear even from the yard.

"He's gone," Aggie told her. "Trish went into town with Morgan, and I told Dusty we decided it would be best not to start until sometime next week. The only people hereabout is you and me. And it doesn't change the fact that you need a man. A good one. And from what I can tell, Dusty McPherson is a good man. One of the best."

"I don't need a man!" Kate paced to the other side of the room. Aggie didn't understand. Oh, she might think Dusty was interested, but Kate knew it was nothing more than a flirtation. She was a passing fancy, and he'd forget about her soon enough, just as soon as he returned to riding bulls and risking his life. It would be different for her, but she would eventually get over it and get on with her life as planned.

"Aunt Aggie," she began, hoping she could make her understand, "I've gotten along without a man for this long. I can do just about anything a man can do. You and I have run this farm just fine since I was fifteen. We may need to hire a little help now and then, but that's all."

Aggie nodded. "Yes, you're a hard worker. I don't think I've ever known a girl to work as hard as you. Except me, maybe," she added with a chuckle. "But it's not for work that you need a man. There won't be farm work in a few weeks."

Kate started to protest, but Aggie held up her hand and continued. "Let me finish. You need a man to love you. To bring out that gentle nature you keep hidden away. It's there, Kate, I know it is. You just don't let anybody but family see it." Her mouth softened to a smile. "I'll bet Dusty's seen it."

Kate sighed, her exasperation getting the best of her. "There's no gentle in me. I'm tough. Besides, you've done fine without a man."

"That was my choice." Hesitating, Aggie stared into her cup as if it held some sort of secret. "I had a man I loved once. And he loved me. But, well, it didn't work out. And no man since then has ever come up to the mark." She looked up at Kate and smiled, a wicked glint in her eyes. "If I were thirty years younger, Dusty would come pretty close, though."

Kate shook her head. "Forget it, Aunt Aggie. Even if you *were* thirty years younger, Dusty isn't in the market for a wife or even a relationship."

Aggie gave an unladylike snort. "If you believe that, you haven't seen the way he looks at you when he thinks nobody's watching."

"You're wrong," Kate denied, her cheeks warming.

"Nope," Aggie argued with a smug smile. "Just observant. He doesn't know it yet, but you're the woman he wants."

"Who says I want *him?*" Kate asked, giving her aunt a hard stare. "Oh, great," she continued when Aggie smiled at her. "Because he looks at me like he wants to—" She couldn't finish. She knew how he looked at her. She'd seen it. And more. And she knew what that look did to her. "No. I can't accept that. That's nothing but sex, and that's all."

Aggie leaned across the table, staring her down. "Are you going to stand there and tell me he doesn't make your heart flutter when you look at him?"

"That's exactly what—" Kate closed her eyes, counting to five, and then she sighed. "Oh, all right," she said, opening her eyes again. "I admit I'm attracted to him. Are you satisfied?"

"Nope," Aggie replied with ease. "Not until he's caught you."

"He's not chasing me!" Kate heard the lie in her own words. Dusty was doing something. She just didn't know what it was, and she suspected he didn't either. "Forget it, Aunt Aggie, and face the truth. You're stuck with me for the rest of your life."

Aggie smiled serenely after taking a drink of coffee. "As pleasant as that thought is to me, it's not gonna happen." Her eyes lost their sparkle. "If you don't want Dusty, and I'm having a real hard time believing that, then that's that. But I have a request."

"What kind of request?" Kate asked, not trusting what her aunt might ask of her.

Aggie's eyes narrowed as if considering something. "You need to get out more. Have fun. Spend time with other people. You've kept pretty much to yourself since you and Trish came to live here. I suspect you kept to yourself even when you were in college. That worries me. Everybody should have friends."

"I have friends." But Kate knew those were few and far between. Except for her aunt and sister, there wasn't anyone she spent time with on a regular basis, sharing her thoughts and dreams and fears.

"You keep lying to yourself like that, and you'll regret it later." Picking up her cup, Aggie walked to the sink and rinsed it. Turning to Kate again, she smiled. "Give yourself a chance. Get out among people. That's all I'm asking."

Kate opened her mouth to argue, but she immediately closed it. Maybe Aunt Aggie was right. Even Dusty had said she needed to broaden her horizons and get some perspective. If it was true that her problem in knowing how to deal with him was because she lacked experience, then maybe that's what she needed to get.

"Okay."

Aggie stared at her. "Really?"

Kate nodded, feeling more certain by the second. "Yes. I *do* need to get out and meet people." Men, to be precise. Maybe then she could learn whatever it was she needed to learn, especially how to deal with Dusty. "So how do I do that?"

Aggie's smile said it all. "Go find Trish. If anybody knows what to do, she does. And she can help with your hair and makeup."

Kate thought of all the times her sister had offered but been turned down. She smiled, too, thinking of how excited Trish would be.

"This just might warrant a trip to Oklahoma City for some new clothes," Aggie said, looking Kate over from head to foot.

Kate knew a little makeup and a new hairdo and clothes wouldn't change anything, but she was willing to give it a try. Besides, it would be a welcome distraction, and she would have something to think about besides how to fight her feelings for Dusty, especially knowing he wouldn't be around much longer.

At the end of the week, after a marathon shopping trip and countless hours with Trish, Kate stood in front of the mirror, staring at her reflection. She nearly didn't recognize the woman looking back at her.

Her hair was free of the braid she always wore, and it flowed over her shoulders and down her back in soft waves. The makeup Trish had so patiently applied brought out Kate's eyes and lips, and the dress they'd chosen could only be described as a dream. Orange, purple and hot-pink flowers flowed around her hips and thighs, while the deep ruffle of the off-the-shoulder bodice showed off her tan. The matching ruffle at the hem didn't come close to the top of her knees, causing her legs to appear miles long.

"What now?" she asked, catching her aunt's pleased expression.

"Two words," Aggie replied. "Blue Barn."

Kate let out a groan and closed her eyes. She really would be getting a whole new experience.

DUSTY DIDN'T KNOW WHY he let Miss Aggie talk him into doing something so crazy. He had seen her at the café with Hettie Lambert while he was having a late supper, and he had wished Kate had been with them. Aggie must have sensed something, because she had told him he looked like he probably needed to relax and have a little fun. He couldn't argue with that, which was why he now found himself sitting at the bar in the Blue Barn.

The honky-tonk was several miles outside of Desperation and not only drew every wannabe cowboy in the county, but also every male out looking for a good time. Female, too, he decided, glancing around at the crowd. A den of iniquity, his grandmother would have called it. He had to agree. He'd been in hundreds of bars, taverns and anything resembling the same from Washington to Florida. None of them beat the Blue Barn for sheer lack of class.

Dark in all the right places, the room reminded him of a huge cavern. Pinpoints of light touched down here and there like fingers pointing. Small, round tables circled the outer perimeter where couples met and couldn't be seen. As a kid, he'd heard stories of what went on. It had been the perfect place to rendezvous with a girl with a well-known lack of virtue. Dusty couldn't count the number of times he'd made plans of his own to sneak into the place and do what came naturally. But it had never happened. He smiled, deciding it was probably a good thing. He'd been wild enough as it was, taking off soon after his high school graduation to elope and make his mark in rodeo. The first had been a major mistake, but rodeo had served him well, until a bull had gotten the better of him.

"Dusty McPherson?"

He turned at the sound of his name to see a slightly familiar face peering at him. The man standing next to him looked to be about his age, but the probably once-slender body had spread, and the face was beginning to bear lines of age.

He looked a little closer. "Jimmy Tartelli?" he asked as recognition hit him.

A broad smile broke out on the man's face. "It's me. Best tight end Desperation High ever had." He slapped Dusty on the back as he settled on the bar stool next to him. "I heard you were back home again. Doug Simpson said he'd been by your place and noticed you'd been doing some work on it. But I sure didn't expect to see you here."

"I hadn't expected to be here," Dusty said, shrugging his shoulders. And he chuckled as memories of high school flooded his mind. Good times, bad times, wild times, he and Jimmy had shared them all.

"I heard you've done well, Dusty. You've made Desperation proud."

Dusty shook his head. "I just ride bulls, Jimmy. Nothing hundreds of other cowboys don't do."

"You were in the Professional Bull Riders Finals a few years back. Only one other person in Desperation can say they've made it that far where rodeo is concerned," his friend pointed out.

"Yeah, Tanner did great last year at National Finals Rodeo and brought home the gold buckle. Too bad I didn't do better in PBR," Dusty admitted.

"You did fine by our standards," Jimmy assured him.

Dusty cocked an eyebrow at him and grinned. "That's not saying much, is it?"

Jimmy threw his head back and laughed. People around them turned to stare, several with looks of recognition in their eyes. Within minutes, Dusty found himself surrounded by several old friends and acquaintances, all pleased to see him.

Feeling relaxed and welcome after everyone but Jimmy drifted away, Dusty swiveled around on the stool and leaned back against the edge of the bar. The dance floor in the middle of the room twinkled with tiny colored lights. Loud music echoed and bounced off the walls from the live band that drew the crowds every weekend.

"The band sure is good," he commented.

"Ted Haverly's one of the band members. Folks come from all over the county to listen to them." Jimmy turned around, too, and the two men sat side by side, enjoying the music.

Dusty remembered Ted and had never liked him much, but he had to admit the band played great and sure knew how to work the crowd. The dance floor never emptied. He sat, beer in hand, and let the music go to his head. Closing his eyes, his mind filled with country strains and memories of the past.

"Well, I'll be," Jimmy exclaimed softly.

Dusty barely heard him. "What?"

"I never thought I'd see the day one of Agatha Clayborne's nieces would show up here."

Dusty's eyes flew open as he jerked upright, nearly toppling from the bar stool. "Clayborne?" he croaked.

"Hey, Dusty, didn't I hear you were working for Miss Aggie a while back?"

Searching through the crowd, Dusty nodded. "Still am."

"Can't you see her?"

"Who?" Dusty couldn't see much of anything through the wall of bodies between them and the dance floor.

But before Jimmy answered, Dusty found her. And he thought the earth had opened up to suck him into its bowels. His mouth went cotton dry, his heart thudded in a too-rapid beat. His hands were suddenly damp, and he wiped them on the legs of his jeans.

In a small space on the dance floor, Kate moved to the music. But it wasn't a Kate like Dusty had ever seen before or even imagined seeing. If it hadn't been for the wild mass of thick, curly copper hair flying behind her, he would have denied it was her. He'd never seen her in a dress, never thought much about it. She always dressed in blue jeans—tight, hip-hugging denim—and shirts that barely whispered femininity, except to hug her body, and that probably only served for practicality. This Kate, this tantalizing woman spinning in a soft, flowing dress that curled and swirled around her with each move she made, nearly stopped his heart.

"Dusty?" Jimmy's voice sounded miles away. "Dusty, you okay?"

Without knowing he'd moved, Dusty found himself on his feet. Forcing air back into his lungs, he nodded, never taking his eyes off Kate as he walked in her direction.

Cool, he ordered himself. It wasn't like him to be out of control.

As the fast-paced song ended, he reached her and watched as she smiled at her partner. The face of the man she'd been dancing with didn't even exist in Dusty's vision. All he saw was Kate.

The band moved into a slow, romantic ballad. Without saying a word, Dusty's arm slid around her waist. At his touch, she jumped and turned, the smile still on her face. But when her gaze made contact with his, her smile vanished and her eyebrows drew together in a frown.

"Dusty," she said, and glanced around as if looking for an escape.

He didn't care if she wanted to dance with him or not. It didn't have anything to do with what she wanted. Turning her into his arms, he held her, and only for a moment did she hesitate. Swaying to the music, she put her arms around his neck, bringing her even closer, and her scent enveloped him. When he looked down and found her gazing up at him, the sensation of teetering on the edge of a bottomless pool overwhelmed him. It wouldn't take much to fall to a sure death by drowning, but he couldn't stop looking at her.

He was certain he'd gone to heaven. Or hell, considering what he was feeling. Another long glance told him she was experiencing something, too. Passion darkened her eyes, but a light within them kept him from getting completely lost. It was crystal clear that giving in to the urge he was feeling would be the end of him.

Before the song ended, he led her off the dance floor. If he had a say in it, she wouldn't be dancing with anyone else the rest of the night. But he knew if he danced with her again he'd fall so hard he'd never recover. And that couldn't happen.

KATE HAD NEVER BEEN so speechless in her life. All thought, except a possible means of escape, had deserted her the moment she'd turned to find Dusty on the dance floor, his arm around her and his eyes full of something she didn't dare label. She knew she should resist, but as he led her to the edge of the room, where light barely existed, she discovered she couldn't. Just once, she wouldn't consider the consequences. Just once, but never again.

They circled the perimeter of the room, but all the tables were filled with couples, heads together, arms around each other, oblivious to everything and everyone. Something deep inside her yearned for intimacy, but the rest of her denied it.

After a second time around the room, Dusty found a deserted corner and led her to it. He leaned against the wall and pulled her close. "What's a nice girl like you doing in a place like this?" he asked her, his all-too-familiar grin tugging at her stuttering heart.

Her common sense returned immediately. "The same thing everyone else is doing." She placed her hands on his chest to ease away, but only managed an inch or two. "I'm having a good time."

"Me, too."

The intensity in his eyes scared her. "Maybe I should say I *was* having a good time."

"Now don't be mean," he said, chuckling, and pulled her close again.

"I'm serious, Dusty." The world had stopped for one short song, replaced by a fantasy. Now that it was over, reality had returned. "I'm not trying to be mean, but you were the last person I expected to see here."

His eyes widened. "Then you can imagine how I felt seeing *you* here. But now that you are…" His hands moved over her back, sending waves of longing rushing along their touch. His breath caressed her ear. His sigh was ragged and torn. "You shouldn't have worn that dress. You don't have a clue…"

She fought the desire that kept building deep inside her—a desire she didn't want to acknowledge, because she knew where it would lead. "It's only a dress, Dusty, just like other women wear. No big deal."

"To you, maybe, but—" He shook his head, looked at her, and shook his head again. "Hon, we have to put a stop to this."

His words said one thing, but he pulled her closer, and when his mouth claimed hers, Kate couldn't stop herself from responding. It was as if she'd lost all control over herself, except for a tiny voice in her head telling her that it wasn't worth the pain of a broken heart.

When they drew apart, Dusty's breathing was ragged. A shaking hand touched her cheek, and even in the dark she could see the desire in his eyes.

"I can't do this. You understand that, don't you?" he asked.

Kate knew. She didn't want to think about it, but she had to. Dusty had made his choice. It wasn't her, no matter what was happening between them. Oh, he wanted her. Aggie had been right about that. He wanted her, and she was his, heart and soul. But she didn't fit into his life, and he would never fit into hers.

"I think I'll go on home now," she told him, knowing she couldn't take being near him any longer. She pulled away, but he stopped her.

"We need to talk about this."

"There's nothing to talk about," she told him, pushing gently at his chest.

He released her with obvious reluctance. "I'll take you home."

She refused to look at him. "I drove."

"I'll walk you out to your truck, then," he insisted.

"Maybe you should just stay here."

"No. Let me do this."

A strong wind blew her hair across her face as they stepped out of the noisy honky-tonk, and she shoved it back, angry at the twists life took. In fairy tales, they'd have declared their love and lived happily ever after. In real life, she had to walk away, knowing that although she was falling for him, she wasn't what he wanted.

When they reached her truck, Dusty backed her against the cab and pressed his forehead to hers. "I never meant for this to happen."

"Don't worry about it, Dusty."

"If I've hurt you—"

"I'll get over it."

He hesitated before he stepped back, releasing her. She stepped out from between him and the truck, and without a glance at him, she climbed into the cab. "I guess I'll see you next week."

He held the edge of the door, keeping her from closing it. "You'll be okay?"

Turning her head, she gathered every ounce of strength she had and looked at him. Ignoring the regret in his eyes, she forced a smile. "I'll be fine. I always am."

DUSTY WATCHED as the taillights disappeared down the dirt road, the dust clouding his view. His heart ached. He admitted that much. Whether he wanted Kate or not wasn't a question he could afford to answer. Determination and single-mindedness had won him more than his share of competitions. And he had the buckles and prize money to prove it. He would learn to get over her. Those same qualities that had led him through his life in the past would take him the rest of the way. If only Kate could be a part of it.

Chapter Eight

Opening his eyes carefully to the sunshine pouring in the windows of his bedroom, Dusty winced at the pain. The headache had come on after Kate had left him in the parking lot of the Blue Barn. He'd gone back inside and hung around for a while, talking to Jimmy and a few others, hoping he could wipe out the memory of Kate's kisses and how her eyes had glowed with passion.

He moved his head, wincing again at the pain. How had he let it go so far? He'd scared her off, which was the last thing he'd wanted to do.

A glance at the clock by his bed told him he'd better get moving, headache or no headache. Retrieving the bottle of pills the doctor had prescribed, he took two, showered and dressed quickly. He'd told Jimmy he'd meet him at the local tavern at eleven. Lou's Place had become famous for its barbecued beef sandwiches, and Dusty hadn't yet had the pleasure of trying one.

The parking lot at Lou's was already filling up when Dusty pulled in. Inside, he found Jimmy at a table, ordered a glass of iced tea and joined him.

"You look like hell," Jimmy said in greeting.

Dusty pulled up a chair and sat across the table from him. "I feel like hell."

"Woman trouble," Jimmy commented with a knowing nod.

"Trouble is putting it mildly," Dusty snorted. "Are you married?"

Jimmy smiled. "Terry Adams. For ten years."

"She lets you go to the Blue Barn?"

Laughing, Jimmy nodded. "Once or twice a year. It stops the itch, and then I don't need to do it again for a long time."

"I can understand that. What's she like?" Dusty asked, seriously wanting to know. "I remember Terry back in school. Pretty girl. Everybody liked her."

"Everybody still likes her," Jimmy boasted. "She's involved in all those women things here in Desperation. Bible school teacher, soloist in the choir, belongs to the Extension Homemakers group, PTA mom for the kids. You know."

Dusty nodded. "A real lady. Can she change the oil in her car?"

Jimmy's eyebrows raised. "Well, now, I doubt she can." His eyes narrowed in thought. "She probably could if somebody showed her. She picks up on things pretty quick."

"Bet she wears dresses," Dusty mumbled.

Jimmy was silent for a moment. "Something tells me this has to do with Kate Clayborne."

Dusty didn't answer. The whole thing had gotten too complicated to explain. He couldn't even sort out his feelings anymore.

"Everybody around these parts wondered how Agatha

Clayborne would do with two teenage girls." Jimmy stopped and laughed quietly. "Looks like she proved to all the old hens that she could do a better job than most."

"Miss Aggie's a good woman."

"Yep. Can't argue with that. Still keeps to herself pretty much, but those girls have made some changes in her. Anyway, I can remember the first time I laid eyes on those two nieces of hers. Took my breath away, let me tell ya."

Dusty let his grin have its way. He hadn't forgotten what Kate had looked like when the girls moved in with Aggie and started attending Desperation High. "Even with Kate's chopped up hair?"

Jimmy laughed. "Even then. I thought about asking Trish out one time, but then Terry and me hooked up. And there's something else I remember."

"What's that?"

"Well, now, it was at one of the community Christmas dinners, maybe after you'd left," Jimmy went on. "You remember those, don't you? Everybody brings something to eat. Covered dish, I think they call it."

Dusty nodded. He remembered the last one he'd been to, his senior year in high school. At the time, he'd only gone to make his grandparents happy. All he'd been able to think about at the time was how long it was until he'd be out of school.

Jimmy had that faraway look in his eyes. "Boys and full-grown men were swarming around those two girls like flies around a honey dipper. Kate's hair was grown out by then, and Trish, she was passing out fried chicken." Jimmy chuckled again. "I had me a piece of that. Melts in your mouth."

"Yeah, I know," Dusty replied.

"You talking about Kate Clayborne's fried chicken?" a new voice piped in.

Dusty looked up to see Ted Haverly pull up a chair. "I saw you dancing with Kate at the Blue Barn last night," Ted said as he joined them.

Dusty didn't have a comment. All he wanted to do was stop thinking about it.

"Don't believe I've ever seen her looking so good," Ted said.

Dusty looked up, feeling a frown. "That so?"

"She comes by here a couple times a week," he explained. "Brings the food Lou serves."

"Which reminds me," Jimmy said, standing. "Should be about time for a delivery. We'd best get our order in before the rush."

Dusty didn't want to miss what Ted had to say about Kate, so he stopped Jimmy. "Would you order me a couple?"

"Sure thing."

When Jimmy had gone, Ted turned to Dusty. "You got something going with Kate? I mean, I saw you two dancing and then walk off the dance floor together."

"No," Dusty quickly answered. But he noticed an interested glint in Ted's eyes. "Not exactly," he added.

"It was a real surprise to see her at the Blue Barn. She doesn't get around much."

"You keep an eye on her, do you?" Dusty asked, feeling a knot form in his stomach.

"Me?" Ted asked, laughing. "I keep an eye on every available woman around these parts. Some more than others. Kate, for instance. She's one feisty lady."

Dusty's fingers tightened around his glass. "Ever take her out?" The idea of Kate with Ted Haverly made his teeth ache.

"Never even asked her," Ted admitted. "I don't think anybody around here has, as far as I know, at least not for a long time. Most everybody was more interested in her sister. Until she got engaged to the sheriff, of course. Kate has pretty much kept herself out on that farm. That's why it was such a shock seeing her last night. It isn't what I'd expect, that's for sure."

Dusty silently reminded himself that he didn't have any plans as far as Kate was concerned.

"I'm glad to see Kate out and about," Ted continued. "Maybe I'll give her a call after all."

Dusty gritted his teeth at the surge of anger that went through him. Kate deserved better than a womanizer like Ted. And if he could stop it— Oh, hell, it wasn't any of his business.

Jimmy returned to the table and took his seat. "Terry's a good cook, but I have to have one of those sandwiches at least once a week."

Lou, the tavern owner, walked over, his caterpillar eyebrows arched over steely eyes. "You sticking to tea, Dusty?"

Dusty looked up at him. "Something wrong with that?"

Lou shrugged his shoulders and refilled the glass from the pitcher he held. "Guess not. If that's what suits you," he said before going back to the bar.

"I didn't figure you to be a teetotaler," Ted said.

Dusty didn't figure it was any of Ted's business, but he answered anyway. "I'm on meds for a rodeo injury."

Ted shrugged and pushed away from the table.

"Whatever. Guess I'll be on my way. You've given me courage, Dusty. I think I might take a chance and ask that redhead out."

Dusty counted to ten to keep from saying something he knew he'd regret. What Kate did was none of his business. He didn't have a stake on her. "Whatever suits you," he managed to mumble.

"Bet she turns him down," Jimmy said when the other man stood and headed for the door.

"Don't count on it," Dusty answered.

Jimmy took a drink of beer, then put the glass down. "Don't pay any attention to Ted," he offered. "He's always thought a lot of himself when it came to the ladies. They don't think much of him though."

Dusty looked to the door where Ted had left. "Doesn't much matter."

"You sure about that?" Jimmy asked. "It wasn't hard to miss you and Kate last night. I thought—well, like you said, it doesn't matter. But if I was a single man…"

"Go on," Dusty urged when Jimmy didn't finish.

Clearing his throat, Jimmy gave Dusty an uneasy smile. "You haven't asked for my opinion, but I think you might want to hear it. Don't know if it'll help or not, though. Just one man's observations."

"You might as well speak up," Dusty answered with a shrug. "Not that it'll help."

"Maybe not," Jimmy agreed, "but it's worth a shot. The thing is, I'd take Kate over her sister, any day." He leaned closer. "Terry may not be able to change the oil or any of that, but when it comes right down to it, she's got her own streak of independence." He tipped back in his chair. "I kinda like that in a woman. But that's just my taste, I guess."

Dusty didn't tell him that it was what had caught his eye about Kate, too.

"I may be wrong," Jimmy added, "but it seems you kinda like Kate."

Dusty shrugged his shoulders. "I'd be lying if I said I didn't like her."

"But that's it?"

"Maybe. Maybe not." He glanced up from the depths of his glass of tea to see Jimmy studying him. "It's more complicated than that."

"Isn't everything?"

Rubbing a hand over his unshaven face, Dusty nodded. He couldn't put a name to what it was he felt for Kate. Even if he could, it wouldn't make a difference. But the last thing he wanted to do was hurt her, and that's where it seemed to be heading.

KATE TURNED the pickup into the parking lot of Lou's Place and searched for a parking placc. *Just my luck,* she thought, before she spied a spot not far from the entrance and pulled into it. With a sigh of exhaustion from yet another sleepless night, she climbed out of the pickup, walked to the back of it and dropped the tailgate. Reaching for the cooker full of barbecued beef, she dragged it to the edge. Couldn't someone be around to help her with the heavy pan for a change?

"Let me give you a hand," a voice behind her said, as if her request had been heard.

She turned to see Ted Haverly, who played in the band at the Blue Barn. Seeing the glint in his eyes, she nearly refused him, but the cooker held more than usual and it had taken both her and Aggie to get it into the truck.

"Thanks," she said, stepping aside.

Ted hefted the heavy cooker and followed her to the building. "A favor for a favor?" he asked before she opened the door.

The question put her on her guard. She'd seen Ted watching her in the past, but she had always managed to avoid him. His reputation didn't endear him to her at all.

"Like what?" she asked, unable to avoid him this time.

"I thought maybe we could go to the Blue Barn some evening when I'm not playing and get to know each other a little better."

Her first instinct to tell him to go to blazes faded as she considered the invitation. She could handle Ted with no problem. Dusty was the one who gave her problems. "Maybe," she told him with a small smile.

The cooker nearly slid from his hands. "Yeah?" he asked, righting it.

"Yeah."

His surprise turned to a broad smile that began to resemble a leer. "We've got gigs until later next week. Maybe then?"

Kate knew she'd lost her mind, but at that moment she didn't care. It was past time she got out and enjoyed herself. In fact, she had been having fun the night before, until Dusty showed up and turned everything upside down.

"I think I can arrange it," she told him as she pulled on the door and held it open for him.

She stepped into the tavern without looking around

and led him to the little room Lou referred to as a kitchen. Ted set the cooker where she instructed, waiting while she plugged it in and made certain everything was all right.

She had started for the door into the tavern, to find Lou and let him know the barbecued beef had arrived, when Ted stopped her, his hand on the door frame, barring her way with his arm. "I promise to show you a real good time."

"I'm sure you think you will," she replied. *Or die trying.* Still, she had to start somewhere, even if it was what she considered to be the bottom of the barrel as far as Desperation men were concerned.

Her remark brought a frown from him as she ducked under his barrier and walked through the doorway. Much to her dismay, he caught up with her and draped his arm across her shoulders. "I do know how to treat a lady," he boasted.

Kate reached up and deftly removed his hand as it inched lower. "This lady is a little different." She gave him a flashy smile. "Slow it down, cowboy, or the Blue Barn is off."

"Whatever you say," he answered, removing his arm with a shrug and a grin.

"Hey, Ted," someone on the other side of the room called out. "Jack says you need some practice on that guitar."

Ted tipped his hat to Kate. "See you later. I gotta go straighten out Jack."

Breathing a sigh of relief, Kate searched for Lou's familiar bald head, finally finding him cleaning a table. But out of the corner of her eye she saw Dusty, sitting at another table nearby. She couldn't make out who was at the table with him, but it didn't matter. He was there, and she needed to find a way to talk to Lou but not him. There was no getting around it though, so she could only hope Dusty wouldn't notice her.

She finally reached Lou without her presence being detected and tapped him on the shoulder, making sure she kept her back to the spot where Dusty was sitting. Lou spun around, making her jump, but luckily she bit the inside of her cheek to keep from letting out a yelp.

His thick eyebrows drew together in a frown, but when he saw who it was, it disappeared. The Claybornes were a cash cow. "Everybody knows not to sneak up on me," he growled. "You bring the sandwich stuff?"

"Don't I always?"

"Yeah, you do. I appreciate it."

She nodded her acknowledgement, but didn't say how much she and her aunt appreciated it. Cooking brought in extra money when they needed it the most. "I'll see you again on Wednesday."

Keeping her back to Dusty's table, she started for the door, still hoping to sneak out without being seen.

"Aren't you going to say hello, Kate?"

Damn. She was only a few steps from escape. Wasn't it enough that she'd had to deal with Ted?

"Kate?"

Taking a deep breath, she turned around and looked directly at Dusty so there would be no mistake. "Hello, Dusty," she said, and then turned back around.

"Whoa! What's your hurry?"

Wishing she had the power to make herself vanish into thin air, she faced him again.

He said something to the man sitting next to him, before flashing her a wide grin. "Come on over and be neighborly. Somebody wants to say hi to you."

"This is insane," she muttered under her breath, but she gave a smile her best shot and walked over to the table. "Hi, Jimmy," she said, when she recognized Dusty's friend. "How's Terry?"

"Mighty fine," Jimmy answered.

"Glad to hear it. Tell her hello from me."

"I'll do that."

Dusty leaned forward. "Have a seat. We're waiting on our orders."

Except for the intensity she saw in his eyes, she would have thought she was an old friend of his and nothing at all had happened the night before. "I need to be getting home."

"Just for a few minutes," he coaxed. "No harm in that, is there?"

She looked around the room, hoping for some other means of escape, other than the main door. "Well…" she said, stalling for the slight chance of a miracle saving her.

The empty chair next to Dusty scooted out from the table, obviously launched by his foot. "What brings you to Lou's Place on a Saturday?" he asked.

Glancing at Jimmy as she sat on the chair, she tried for a smile. "It's delivery day."

Jimmy looked at Dusty. "Remember me telling you that she comes by twice a week and today was one of 'em?"

"Oh, yeah," he said, without his gaze ever leaving her. "I forgot. I thought maybe you came in to cuddle up with that cowboy in the doorway."

She knew exactly what he was referring to, and fury shot through her. "I was *not* cuddled up with anybody."

"Suit yourself." The smile on his face looked suspiciously like a sneer.

Jimmy's chair screeched on the wood floor when he scooted it back. "You know, I think I'll go get those sandwiches and leave you two to…whatever."

When Dusty didn't bother to reply, Kate knew she was in trouble. "I think it's time for me to leave," she said, starting to stand.

Dusty put his hand on her wrist and kept her from moving. "Oh, no, you don't. Running away isn't going to help."

They stared at each other in silence for what seemed like ten minutes, but Kate knew was only a few seconds. She noticed his eyes weren't as bright as they usually were, and there seemed to be a decided strain in the planes of his face. "You look like something the cat wouldn't bother to drag in."

"Thanks."

"And you were extremely rude about that thing with Ted."

"I suppose I should apologize."

"It certainly wouldn't hurt."

He removed his hand and leaned back in his chair. "Okay, I was out of line with that remark."

She rubbed her wrist and saw something flash across his face. A brief frown? Concern that he might have hurt her? Or something else?

"Tell me about the deliveries," he said.

"There's nothing to tell," she answered with a shrug. "I bring the barbecued beef on Saturdays and

Wednesdays. Aggie takes the pies to the café and I cover Lou's Place."

His gaze never left her. It felt as if he could see into her and knew what she was thinking. What she was feeling.

"I thought you said making a business of your cooking would kill the fun of it."

"It would," she said through gritted teeth. Why did he insist on talking about it? He wouldn't discuss his bull riding with her, so why should she discuss this or the farm or her accounting business with him?

"But isn't that what you're doing?" he asked.

"No. It isn't full time."

"I don't see the difference."

Standing quickly, she shoved her chair back under the table. "That's your problem."

"Kate!"

But she was halfway to the door, determined never to let him question her again. About anything.

Chapter Nine

Kate looked up from the biscuits she was cutting to see Trish enter the kitchen. "Want some coffee?" Kate asked, glancing at the clock. It was much too early for her sister to be up. And she was worried. She thought she had heard Trish crying during the night.

Walking to the window, Trish shook her head. "Maybe later."

Kate went back to rolling the biscuit dough, unsure whether she should ask Trish what was bothering her. Even though they were worlds apart in temperament and likes and dislikes, they'd always been close, but there had been changes since Trish and Morgan had become engaged. Not that Kate minded. Nobody could be happier for her sister than she was. But she didn't like the idea that something—or someone— had made Trish cry.

"I've been asked to go on a tour to promote my book this fall."

Kate's hands stilled on the rolling pin. "Trish, that's fantastic! What a great opportunity for you."

Trish turned around and took her seat at the table

where Kate was working. "I can't tell you how surprised I was when my publisher called yesterday."

Dusting off her hands, Kate sank to her own chair, excited at the news. "Why didn't you tell us? Where will you go? Just around here? Oklahoma City? How long will you be gone?"

Trish folded her hands on the table in front of her. "So many questions! I'll go to New York first to meet with my publisher, then a six-week tour of major cities in the East and Midwest. Depending on how that goes, there may be another tour after the first of the year, traveling farther west."

Kate was speechless. "Wow. Six weeks. They must be really impressed with your children's book, not that I blame them. It's a beautiful story."

"They certainly seem to be impressed."

Kate noticed Trish wasn't as excited as she was, but blamed it on her sister's modesty. "So when do you leave?"

Before Trish could answer, Aggie shuffled into the kitchen, her blue chenille robe belted tightly around her. "There's nothing I hate more than mornings," she grumbled.

Trish jumped up from her chair. "Let me get you some coffee. You sit down."

Aggie nodded and gave her a grateful smile. "This old body just loves a night of sleep, but it sure does ache the next morning. And with rain moving in—"

"Rain?" Kate asked. She hated storms, but even worse, Dusty was expected in a couple of hours to help with the machinery. If it rained, she feared Aggie might ask him to stick around until it quit, and that meant sitting here in the kitchen keeping him company.

"Maybe," Aggie said, "although I don't think it was in the forecast for today." She patted Kate's shoulder as she passed by on her way to the window. "The sun is shining, but the air is so heavy, I wouldn't be surprised." She slowly lowered herself to her chair and sighed. "We're in no hurry though, so a little rain won't hurt."

Kate nodded. There was no rush to get the machinery ready to sell or send to auction. Especially not for her. She'd done everything she could to figure out a way to keep her aunt from leasing the farmland, but she'd come up empty-handed. She still held a small bit of hope, but even that was slipping each day she continued to crunch the numbers with no new results.

"Have you heard Trish's news?" she asked, needing to change the subject to something less depressing.

Aggie looked up at Trish as she set a cup of coffee in front of her. "What news is that?"

"Her publisher is sending her on a book tour," Kate answered for her sister.

"A tour?" Aggie asked.

Trish returned to her seat and nodded, then repeated what she'd told Kate. "I'll have to take some time off from teaching, but if it helps sell some books, it's worth it."

"Not to mention seeing all those new places," Aggie added. "I always wanted to travel, but Chicago was the farthest I ever got."

Kate turned to look at her. "I never knew you went to Chicago."

"I lived there for two years," Aggie said.

"Really?"

Nodding, Aggie got to her feet and picked up her coffee cup. "But that was a long time ago. Things have changed, so I doubt it's the Chicago I remember." She turned to Trish. "You enjoy every minute of your trip. Don't let them keep you from seeing all the sights."

Both girls stared after her as she walked out of the kitchen. Kate turned to her sister when she was sure her aunt was out of hearing range. "I wonder if that's where she met the love of her life."

Trish's eyes widened. "Love of her life?"

"Yeah. The guy she left behind. The romance that didn't work out. Has she ever told you about it?"

"I've never heard a thing," Trish said, shaking her head. "How do you know?"

Shrugging, Kate scooted her chair back and stood. "She mentioned it to me a week or so ago." She quickly explained what Aggie had told her, skipping over the rest of the conversation they'd had and going back to her biscuits. "It sure surprised me."

"No kidding. That's…wow."

"She's afraid I'll never get married," Kate said, banging the rolling pin on the dough a little harder than usual. "Not that I want to ever get married." When she looked up at Trish, her sister's head was bowed and her shoulders were shaking. "Trish?" She left the rolling pin and the dough and went to put her arms around her sister. "What is it?"

"It's M-Morgan," Trish whispered and then sniffed.

Kate felt a wave of dread sweep over her. "What's he done?"

Trish shook her head. "Nothing yet. But—"

Kate took the chair beside her and reached for her hands. They were cold. "Tell me."

Nodding, Trish took a deep breath. "I told him about the tour yesterday. I was so excited that they want me to do this, and I thought he would be, too." She turned to look at Kate. "It'll start in late October."

"October?" Kate asked. "But your wedding is set for October."

Trish's eyes filled with tears. "There may not be a wedding."

"What?"

"I asked Morgan if we couldn't postpone the wedding until after the holidays. After all, the invitations haven't been printed yet, and there's no reason we can't get the church then."

"And he said no?"

"He threatened to cancel it, if I go on the tour."

Kate couldn't ever remember feeling so angry at anyone. Even when her aunt had told her about leasing the land, she hadn't felt like tearing her head off, but that's exactly what she wanted to do to Sheriff Morgan Rule. "He can't do that."

Tears spilled from Trish's eyes when she nodded. "Yes, he can." When Kate started to stand, Trish stopped her. "What are you doing?"

"I'm going to have a few words with the sheriff, that's what."

Trish pulled her back down to the chair. "No, Kate. Don't do that. We'll work it out. Somehow."

"And if you don't?"

Trish shook her head and said nothing.

Kate was ready to rip the man apart. As far as she was concerned, he deserved it. But if Trish didn't want her to get involved, she wouldn't. Not yet, anyway.

"All right," Kate said, patting Trish's hand. "But if you need me to straighten him out, you let me know."

And straighten him out she would. If only she could straighten out her own problem. But time, she knew, would do that all on its own. She only had to hang on until Dusty returned to bull riding without doing something foolish. Then she could put Dusty and her memories behind and move on.

THE MINUTE Dusty stepped into the Clayborne kitchen, he knew there was trouble brewing.

"Wipe your feet," Kate said, without turning from the table to look at him.

"Good morning to you, too," he said, doing as he was told.

"Breakfast is over," she continued without moving, "but there's coffee on the counter. You know where the cups are. And there's some biscuits left. Help yourself."

"Where's Aggie?" he asked, moving to pour the coffee. When he had the steaming mug in his hand, he grabbed a biscuit from the plate on the table in front of Kate and took his usual seat next to her.

She shuffled a deck of cards in her hand and started laying out a solitaire game, not even acknowledging he was there.

"It's a nice day," he said, hoping for something more in the way of conversation.

Without losing a beat in her game, she nodded.

"Oh, there you are."

He looked up to see Aggie walking into the kitchen. "Morning, Miss Aggie. It's a good time to get some work done on that machinery. Maybe we can get it done fast enough that you can get started on the ground work."

"That's so," Aggie said, and took her place at the table. She glanced at Kate, who continued to play her card game.

"Ten of diamonds will go there," he said, putting his finger on the jack of clubs.

Aggie cleared her throat, getting his attention. "Do you still lease your farmland to Dick Berger?"

"Until the lease is up next year," Dusty answered, nodding. "But I haven't decided if I'll extend it."

Beside him, Kate made a sound. "Why not?" she asked, but her attention remained on the cards in front of her.

The sound she'd made had been so brief, he wasn't sure what it might have been about. Interest, maybe. It could be she was hoping to lease his farmland. That wouldn't bother him, except he'd had what he thought was a better offer.

"I got a call Saturday afternoon from Red Hill Farms looking to buy it," he explained.

When she turned to look at him, there was no mistaking what was in her eyes. "You can't sell that land," she told him.

Glancing at Aggie, whose face gave away nothing, he smiled. "Of course I can. I own it. I can do whatever I want to with it. And since I won't be around to farm it for a long, long time—"

"You might need it later," Kate reminded him. "You never know what might happen, and you just might need that money from the lease."

"What I get from the sale would more than cover that," he answered. "And I won't have to hassle with paperwork every year for the government or paying my share of the fertilizer bills or the seed wheat bills or the—"

She shoved the cards into a pile and left them. "I can't believe you don't know the real value of land."

"What does that mean?"

Her chair scraped along the floor as she stood. "Your grandparents worked that land for years and years. I doubt when they left it to you they thought you'd be selling it."

He felt an argument coming on and wasn't in the mood for one, but he wasn't going to let her comment go, either. "I don't know what they had in mind, but they gave it to me with no restrictions, so it's mine to do with as I please."

Her chin went up and she strode to the sink, placing her hands on the edge of it. Her back was stiff, and her shoulders moved with each breath she took. Turning around, she glared at him. "The family farm is dying, Dusty, because of corporations like the one you're thinking of selling out to."

"Now wait just a minute," he said, ready to defend a decision he hadn't completely made. "I'm not selling out."

"Are you losing money?"

"That's not the point," he said, trying to keep his voice calm and even.

"You're right. The point is that land is something you don't just give away, especially if it's been in the family for a long time. You do everything you can to keep it."

"Kate—"

"People come and go, Dusty. They move in and out of your life. They *die*. And sometimes they leave you something precious. Something that will be forever. Like land."

Dusty wasn't sure how to answer her. He knew she

loved farming. He'd watched her work harder than anyone throughout all of harvest. He knew it wasn't a hobby for her, but something that meant a lot to her. But he also knew she didn't understand his situation.

He'd heard a rumor that the Clayborne farm was seeing some hard times, and he thought about offering to lease his land to them with the hope it would help. Not knowing their situation, he didn't know if it would solve their problems or make them worse. The only way to find out was to ask.

"Do you want to lease my land, Kate?"

She shook her head. "No, that's not what I want. And I'm surprised you even have the nerve to ask."

Aggie got up from the table and moved to place a hand on Kate's shoulder. But it was Dusty she spoke to. "Kate's not upset with you," she said, ignoring the fierce look Kate gave her. "She's angry with me."

Kate twisted away and moved to the other side of the room, not looking at either of them. There was no doubt she was angrier than he ever remembered seeing her.

"Why?" he asked, looking from one to the other. Kate refused to make eye contact and crossed her arms over her chest. "If I'm asking something I shouldn't, I'm sorry," he said to Aggie.

Aggie sighed and took her seat at the table again. "It'll be no secret soon, if it even is now. I told Kate a few weeks ago that I was planning to lease the farmland to someone. It's getting to be more than she and I can handle, and we're losing more money than we're gaining."

Dusty nodded. He'd heard much the same from others, all over the country. Friends were doing the same in other areas, and it was one more reason why he was considering selling. His current tenant might be in the same situation before long, meaning Dusty would have to find someone else to lease to. Or sell to. At least selling to Red Hill Farms meant he wasn't selling it for a housing development, as some were. It would remain farmland. But he didn't think pointing that out would help. Kate didn't understand that it was possible he'd get more out of it now than later on. It was a business decision for him, and nothing else. For her it was much, much more.

He turned to look at her standing in stony silence on the other side of the room. "I'm sorry, Kate. I know how much farming means to you."

"You have no idea."

"Kate," Aggie said, a warning tone in her voice. Turning to Dusty, she gave an apologetic smile. "I think it would be better today if you'd go on back home. We can start on the machinery tomorrow."

The look on Kate's face was a mixture of relief and pain, but Dusty didn't know how to help. "We'll do whatever needs doing to get it ready for whatever you decide to do," he told Aggie. "Won't we, Kate?"

But Kate didn't answer and, instead, left the kitchen without a word. Dusty knew her heart was breaking and wished he could comfort her in some way. But nothing he could say or do would change the situation.

"TRISH AND I ARE headed into Lawton for parts," Aggie called to Dusty the next day. "We shouldn't be gone long." With a wave, she climbed into the pickup and pulled away.

As soon as he had arrived at the farm, Dusty had gone to drive what Aggie referred to as the "good tractor" around to the machine shed, where it would be closer to the tools they might need to get it in tiptop shape. But the tractor hadn't wanted to start, and after looking it over with Kate's silent help, they discovered there were more than minor repairs that needed to be made on it. He hated that Aggie would have to pour more money into it, but if it wasn't running, it would bring less money in a sale. The cost of parts could make a difference in the profit they could make if it was in good condition.

He had cursed the machine, calling it every obscene name he'd learned over his years on the circuit. It still sat forlornly at the edge of the field adjacent to the house, where they had started other work on it while waiting for the needed parts. His mood hadn't lightened a bit.

He hadn't slept a wink all night, still going over the past few days in his mind. The image of Kate in the dress she'd worn on Friday night at the Blue Barn hadn't dimmed in his mind. The memory of her response to him that night was as fresh as if it had just happened. And the argument the day before about farming still preyed on his mind. The day didn't promise much good.

As the pickup drove out of sight, he cautiously made his way to the tractor where Kate stood, muttering some of the same things he had earlier.

"They'll be back with the parts in no time," he told her, needing to say something.

"Hand me the big wrench," she said without looking up.

He dug through the tool box and finally found it on the ground, then handed it to her. She took it without even a thanks, a glance or a "go jump off a cliff." Tired, his patience with her was wearing thin.

"About the corporation thing—" He couldn't finish. No matter what he said, it would be wrong. "You used to at least talk to me," he grumbled instead.

"I don't have anything to say to you," she answered briefly.

He weighed his next words before speaking. "I'm sorry about Friday night. You just looked so—"

"Forget it."

"I wish I could," he muttered.

The wrench slipped from her hand. "Damn!" she snarled.

He gently moved her aside. "Would you let me do this?" he asked, severely exasperated with her obstinacy. The woman had the biggest stubborn streak of anyone he knew, including his mother. He picked up the heavy wrench where she'd dropped it, and anger filled him. She didn't have any business wrestling tools almost as big as she was.

Feeling her eyes on him, he looked up to find her with her finger in her mouth. "You hurt yourself." He set the wrench down and reached for her hand to take a look at her injury, but she jerked away. "Kate, we need to clean it up."

"I can do it." Turning on her heel, she stalked to the house.

He watched her, feeling angry and powerless at the same time. "Fool," he muttered. By trying to make things better, he'd made them worse, and he hoped he hadn't damaged his friendship with her. Somehow he would find a way to get back to the way things were before the Blue Barn. Even before that first kiss on the porch.

Slipping the wrench back on the part she'd been attempting to loosen, he gave a hard tug. Sweat soaked his T-shirt, but the stubborn bolt finally came free.

By the time she returned he had the part off. He checked her hand without her being aware of it and felt easier when he saw a bandage on her finger.

"I got it off," he pointed out.

She picked up the wrench and put it in the tool box. "Now if they'd just get back with the part."

"It shouldn't be much longer," he assured her. "Aggie called the part number into the dealer before they left. It'll be ready and waiting. They'll be back soon."

Kate fidgeted, looking up at the slowly darkening sky. "I hope you're right."

Dusty followed her gaze. "There's a storm moving in," he commented, noting the dark, heavy clouds moving in quickly from the southwest.

"I know."

Catching the note of fear in her voice, he decided to divert her attention. "Do we need to take this pulley off?"

Kate nodded, taking another glance at the sky. "We'll need the crowbar." She made a move to get it.

"Why don't you let me?" he asked, beating her to it.

"Are you sure you know how?"

With a grin he hoped would take her mind off the weather, he chuckled. "I do, but you can talk me through it anyway if it'll make you feel better."

He knew he'd hit a nerve when her shoulders stiffened. He hadn't meant to but he didn't comment. Positioning the crowbar, he started prying the pulley. He wondered how she ever managed to do it by herself. And wondered, too, why the approaching storm made her so nervous.

"Does Aggie have trouble driving in the rain?" he asked, knowing how protective she was of her family.

Her eyes darted to the sky again, and she shook her head, but she never looked directly at him. "She'll pull off the road if it gets bad. Or she won't start out into it, to begin with. She probably has more sense than I do."

Dusty couldn't argue with that. Kate had obviously learned a lot of things from her aunt, including her muleheadedness, he guessed. But Aggie seemed to have enough sense to know what she shouldn't attempt. Kate always seemed determined to prove something. She didn't need to prove anything to him. He'd seen her do more than a lot of people did and knew she could handle just about anything.

And wear anything. He shoved the memory of her in the dress from his mind.

When Kate shivered in a chill wind that was getting stronger, Dusty longed to wrap his arms around her, but he hesitated to do anything. Gritting his teeth, he gripped the crowbar tighter and pried. The pulley wheel snapped off.

"That's it," Kate said, retrieving the part. Large drops of rain hit them both as she straightened.

"I'll get the crowbar," he told her. As he grabbed for it, the first bolt of lightning flashed in the dark sky. Kate let out a yelp that was drowned out by a deafening clap of thunder. He quickly scaled the tractor ladder and threw the crowbar and toolbox in the cab.

The rain came down in buckets as he scrambled down and hit the ground again. Kate shivered next to him. "Let's get to the house," he shouted.

But Kate stood frozen, staring at the sky as the rain hit her face.

"Kate, come on, let's get inside," he shouted, hoping to get her moving. When it didn't work, he grabbed her hand and tugged. "Let's go, hon. We're getting soaked."

She finally allowed him to pull her along, but she never took her attention from the sky.

He shoved open the door into the kitchen and sent her in ahead of him, closing the door behind him and making sure neither of them slipped on the rain that had blown in with them.

"What's that?" he asked, hearing a long, loud beep.

She stood near the window, watching the blowing rain outside. "It's the storm alert radio."

He found the radio in the hall on a small table and listened to the warning being issued. "It's a thunderstorm warning," he said when he returned to the kitchen. She still stood at the window, and he walked over to her. Outside, the rain came down almost horizontally, making it difficult to see anything.

And then he heard the hail begin to hit the sides of the house. "Come on, Kate, let's get away from the window."

"Just like before," she whispered.

"What?" And then he remembered she had lost her parents in a tornado. "Let's find someplace to wait this out," he told her, hoping this was nothing more than the bad thunderstorm the warning had indicated.

He led her down the hall and into the living room. Looking around, he noticed heavy draperies on the windows. After settling her on the big sofa, he went to close the drapes, in case hail might break the windows. He could still make out the announcements coming from the radio in the hall and listened for word of anything worse than what they were experiencing.

So far, so good. Hopefully there would be only rain and the hail beating down, and maybe that wouldn't last much longer. He winced, thinking of the tractor and the damage that might be done to it, but there wasn't anything he could do.

He sat on the sofa beside her and pulled her close. She was soaked and cold, and he wrapped his arms around her, cradling her and stroking her wet hair. She didn't resist.

The lights flickered twice and then the power went out completely, leaving the room in darkness. The storm radio, obviously running on batteries, continued to issue the warning. "Just like before," she said again.

He wasn't sure it would help, but he wondered if talking about the storm that had taken her parents' lives would help. "How was it then?" he asked.

She turned her head to look at him for a moment, and he saw her close her eyes. "Bad," she said. "Trish and I were at school. She was at the high school and I was in middle school, down the street."

"So you weren't together?"

She shook her head. "We all thought it was a drill." She opened her eyes to look at him again. "Do you remember those?"

"Sure do," he said, trying for a smile. "Out in the hall, on our knees, and bent over facing the wall, our hands clasped at the back of our heads."

"That's it," she said with a shaky smile. "And we heard it outside. The wind, the hail. And then it was quiet, like it was all over, but it only lasted for about half a minute. Then there was a roar."

He didn't want her lingering on the memory. "But the school wasn't hit."

"No, it wasn't. When it was over, they tried to keep us there, but I sneaked away and ran to Trish's school. I knew she'd be scared, and I found her. She was on her way to find me." She stopped for a moment, but continued before he could form words that might comfort her. "We were supposed to stay there. We both knew it. But we only lived a few blocks from the schools, so we started home. And the closer we got, the worse the damage was. We were a block from our house, and we could see trees that were twisted like pretzels and some ripped from the ground. Roofs were torn off. Cars had been tossed here and there. Debris from houses and buildings was everywhere."

"Kate, maybe this isn't a good—"

"No, it's okay," she told him. "It's good to talk about it. I never did."

He realized she had relaxed a little and that the storm outside was letting up. The hail had stopped and the wind had died down some. "Okay," he said. "Whatever you think is best."

She took a deep shaky breath and continued. "We weren't far from our house, and we could see people around it, moving things out of the way. When we got closer, one of the neighbors met us and turned us away from the house. She was crying and hugging both of us, and she said Mom and Dad had been trying to get in the basement, but they didn't make it."

Dusty blinked his eyes, warding off the sorrow he felt for her and her family. "I'm so sorry, Kate."

Turning in his arms, she pressed her hand against his

face. "It's all right, Dusty. Trish and I were very lucky. It could have been worse. The schools might have been hit, and to think of what might have happened then—"

The power returned, and only seconds passed by before they heard a door slam and voices. Dusty eased away from Kate, made certain she was all right and started for the kitchen.

"There you are," Aggie cried when he reached the entry hall. "We saw the lights go on when we drove up. Is Kate all right?"

"She was terrified," he said, still a little shaky himself. "That was one hell of a storm. She's in the living room."

Aggie nodded and started down the hall. "She's been terrified of them since she lost her parents. We try to stay with her and help her through it when we can, but we couldn't do it today." She turned back to give him a sad smile. "I'm glad you were here and she wasn't alone. I'm sure it helped."

Unable to speak, he nodded and headed for the door. Feeling as if he'd been sucker punched, he climbed into his pickup and drove home, fighting the muddy roads. When he finally made it to his house, he killed the engine and pressed his forehead against the steering wheel, his fingers still gripping it. His head felt as if it would explode. He knew he should go on into the house and take a couple of pills, but he wasn't able to move. All he could think of was Kate.

He wasn't in love with her. He'd never been in love with anyone. But he was damn close with her.

Chapter Ten

Kate sat at the O'Brien dinner table and wished she hadn't accepted Jules' invitation. If she had known Dusty would be there, too, she would have stayed home and worked on a way to continue farming. Dusty was his usual charming self, but after pouring her soul out to him the day before in the storm, she wasn't interested in spending the evening with him. She was embarrassed for having allowed him to see her biggest weakness. It wouldn't happen again.

Everyone was enjoying the strawberry crêpes dessert she'd brought, and she was flattered that Jules and Tanner considered her a friend, so the evening wasn't turning out as bad as she had feared it would. Jules had assured her on her arrival that she and Tanner weren't matchmaking, but she also admitted it wasn't such a bad idea. Kate had laughed at her honesty. She only wished she could have been more help in persuading Dusty not to return to bull riding. Deep down, she knew he would be leaving soon. She had to accept that, but doing so was becoming more and more impossible by the day. If anything were to happen to him, she would never be able to forgive herself.

"This has been a wonderful dinner," she told Jules as they all began to leave the table.

"Thank you," Jules replied, "but most of the credit goes to Bridey. She's the real cook in the family."

Kate had known Bridey Harcourt, Tanner's aunt, for years. Bridey's stories of her childhood in Ireland were priceless and Kate told her how much she had enjoyed them.

"Probably not nearly as much as I enjoy telling them," Bridey said, laughing. "All of these people have heard them so many times, they can recite them on their own." When the O'Briens and even Dusty assured her she was wrong, her cheeks pinked with pleasure. "I'll never forget the first time I met your aunt, Kate. She helped me pick out the best fabric for a dress I wanted to make. That was when I saw what a giving woman she was and not the least bit shy about it."

Kate's eyes misted, and she smiled and nodded, thinking of all the things Aunt Aggie had done for Trish and her. "If I remember, she has some of your recipes."

"Yes! I gave her some, years ago. Have you tried any of them?"

Kate nodded. "Many of them. But I admit, I've made my own little changes and additions."

Bridey patted her hand. "That's the way a good recipe—and a good cook—gets better."

Dusty moved to stand beside Kate. "You know, Kate, maybe Bridey would be interested in going in on that restaurant idea."

"Restaurant?" Jules asked, looking from Kate to Dusty.

Kate gave Dusty a look that she hoped would stop him. It didn't.

"I suggested to Kate that she should expand on her talent and maybe start a restaurant," he explained to everyone.

"Are you serious about this, Kate?" Jules asked.

"Not in the least," Kate said, hoping her smile appeared authentic. "Dusty knows it, too. Don't you, Dusty?" she said, looking up at him.

"Now, Kate—" But he stopped, the expression on his face clearly showing he understood she meant business. And not cooking business.

She turned to the others, her smile more genuine. "Thank you all again for inviting me. I promised Trish I'd help with some of her wedding details, so I need to get home." It was only a little fib. There was no guarantee there would be a wedding. "So if you'll excuse me…"

"I'll walk you out to your truck," Dusty said, slipping her arm through his.

She wanted to tell him not to, but instead, she thanked her hostess and promised to visit again soon.

Tanner followed them to the front entry. "I have something I'd like to talk with you about, Dusty," he said as Dusty opened the door for Kate.

"Sure," Dusty said. "I won't be *too* long," he added with a grin and a wink. Neither sat well with Kate.

Instead of making something of it, she walked out the door and stepped onto the porch, breathing in the summer night air. Everything would have been perfect if Dusty hadn't insisted on seeing her to her truck. Even a beautiful night couldn't change the fact that Dusty had decided he knew what was best for her.

She waited until he joined her on the porch and

closed the door behind them, and then she turned to look at him. "What is it with you? I told you I didn't want to make cooking a business."

The look on his face was proof that she had taken him by surprise, but he quickly recovered. "But you already have. There's the pies and cakes at the café and the bar-becued beef at Lou's. It already *is* a business. Why not expand it?"

"I don't know why you can't understand," she said, shaking her head, "so let me put it this way. Bull riding is your career, right?"

"Right."

"And you're good at it."

"Very good."

Kate smiled at his certainty in his ability. She wasn't that much different when it came to her farming. "And you enjoy it."

"I wouldn't be doing it if I didn't."

"You mean you wouldn't be risking your life to do it if you didn't." It had come out of her mouth without thinking.

Frowning, he stuffed his hands in his pockets. "I thought we agreed not to talk about that."

"Just making a point," she said, needing to defend her gaffe.

He nodded. "Point taken. At least on that. But I don't see—"

"Let me finish," she said, before she lost her train of thought. "You enjoy working on your house, but would you go into construction if you couldn't ride bulls anymore?"

"No." He took a step closer to her. "Kate, I only want to help. Maybe it hasn't sunk in yet, but Aggie is leasing the land to someone else. That will bring in some money, and you have your accounting business, but it may not be enough. Or am I wrong?"

She dug her fingernails, stubby as they were, into her palms, and said nothing.

"I'm right, aren't I?" he asked, his voice soft and concerned.

"And I suppose that changes things?" Why did this man infuriate her so often and so much?

"You know, you're beautiful when you're mad."

"Stop it!"

"Okay." His grin was heart-stopping.

She closed her eyes and took a deep breath before opening them again. "It's simple, Dusty. I don't want you interfering in my life any more than you want me interfering in yours."

He took a step toward her, but she took two back, and he sighed. "What did I do to lose your trust, Kate?"

"Is that what this is about? Trust?"

"You didn't trust me enough to tell me about the farm. I thought we were friends. I thought we were—" He shook his head and looked past her.

"We were never that."

"I think we still are."

And Kate thought he saw too much. She had believed she was tough, but Dusty had come along and touched something in her that no one else had. He made her want things she'd never wanted before, and then he denied her those things.

"I don't know what you mean," she said, trying her best to maintain what dignity she had left.

"Yeah, you do."

"You seem to think you know me. You don't." She turned to leave.

Dusty reached for her, stopping her. "You're always running away from me. Talk to me, Kate. Tell me something I don't know."

"You don't need to know anything more."

He was studying her intently and then pulled her closer. "What is it you're afraid of, Kate?"

She ached with the need to tell him that she was afraid she would lose him, the same as she had lost her parents. "I'm afraid—"

But she couldn't go on.

He touched her cheek with his hand and looked into her eyes. "What is it, Kate? Let me help."

It was time to put herself out of her misery. Time to go back to life before Dusty. And there was only one way to do that. "If you want to help me—to help all of us—there's one thing you can do."

"What's that?"

"Leave me alone. Leave *us* alone. Stay away," she told him, trying to mean it with all her heart. "We don't need you. *I* don't need you." Instead of waiting for an answer or for him to argue, she turned and hurried down the steps to her truck.

DUSTY WAS STUNNED, unable to move, as he watched Kate drive away. He had only meant to help her and her family, but somehow she had taken it wrong, and she never wanted to see him again. The whole conversation had been crazy. But even crazier, he was hurting.

Knowing he needed to tell Jules and Tanner goodbye, he went back inside the house. "That was a great dinner,

Jules," he said, when he found both O'Briens still in the dining room. "Thanks for inviting me."

"You don't need an invitation, Dusty," Jules told him. "You know that. Now you and Tanner get out of here so I can clean up."

"I can help with that," Dusty offered.

Jules laughed as she stacked the plates on the table. "I'm sure you can, but I'd rather you didn't. Men just seem to get in the way when it comes to kitchen stuff. Not meaning to, of course," she hurried to say.

Dusty grinned at her. "Another independent woman. I'd have never guessed." But his smile disappeared as soon as he turned around to follow Tanner. He was still stinging from Kate's demand that he stay away from her.

"Come on into my office," Tanner was saying. "It's become the last bastion of manhood around here. Even Shawn knows he's safe in here," he said, opening the door to the room. "At least from Jules, that is. Not so much from Rowdy."

Dusty laughed, having witnessed the battles between Shawn and the ranch foreman, and took a seat on the old leather chair facing the massive desk. Tanner opened a wooden box that sat on the desk and offered the contents to Dusty. "Imported, if you want to indulge."

Dusty shook his head at the rows of cigars. "I'll pass."

Circling the desk, Tanner lowered himself to the chair behind it. "I've been wanting to talk to you."

"About what?" Dusty asked, getting comfortable. The way his luck was going, it wouldn't be good.

"I've been toying with the idea of starting a rodeo stock company."

"Sounds interesting and the perfect thing for an old rodeo cowboy."

"*Old* being the operative word," Tanner answered with a chuckle.

"But that wasn't the main reason you quit," Dusty pointed out.

"I *retired*," Tanner said. "The fact is that I knew I was getting too old to get bounced and battered every weekend, even before I met Jules. But I wanted a couple more years to try for the championship. I owed it to myself. And I was lucky enough to retire with a gold championship buckle. That's more than a lot of cowboys can say."

Although Dusty and Tanner had competed in different events at different rodeos and in different organizations, Dusty missed sharing his vocation with his best friend. "So what about this idea of a stock company? Does Jules know about it?"

Tanner shrugged and leaned back. "I've mentioned it to her a couple of times. She doesn't have a problem. For one thing, she's been happy to point out that with my rodeo days over, it would be a good way to stay in it without getting all busted up."

Dusty laughed. "I can see her point, considering. It sounds reasonable to me. So she's all for it?"

"Right now, her hands are pretty full with Wyoming and getting her boys' ranch started. She's been dreaming of it for years."

"That sounds like Jules," Dusty said. "I hope it works out. But back to the subject, you're wanting some pointers from me about stock?"

Tanner shook his head and smiled. "I'm wanting to know if you'd like to be a partner in the company."

Surprised, Dusty wasn't sure what to say, but it didn't take him long to decide. "I'm not retiring. I'll still be riding bulls."

"Don't you think the odds are against you on that? Especially considering your doctor's warning."

"Experience gives me higher odds," Dusty reminded him. "You know that."

"I know you're talking crazy."

"If it wasn't for Jules, you'd still be competing instead of thinking about starting a stock company," Dusty insisted.

"You're wrong," Tanner said. "I offered to quit when I asked her to marry me. She wouldn't let me."

"Then she's an even better woman than I'd thought," Dusty acknowledged. "What about Rowdy? What does he think of all this? After all, he's your ranch foreman."

"Rowdy likes the idea. He'll still manage the regular ranch business. The stock company would be mine. Or mine and yours, if you agree to come in with me on it."

Dusty was tempted. "Full partners?"

"Damn right. I wouldn't have it any other way."

"It sounds great, Tanner," Dusty admitted, and he even seriously considered it. If he could find a way to do both—ride bulls and be involved as a stock contractor—it might be just the ticket.

"Are you thinking of settling down before too long?"

Dusty shook his head, thinking of the stubborn look on Kate's face when she told him she didn't want to see him again. "There's no woman in my future."

Tanner studied him. "Not even the hint of one?"

"None."

"I thought maybe—"

"Don't. It's not going to happen. I'm a bull rider."

"And I was a bronc rider, and it didn't stop me from having a wife and starting a family."

"But you're, you know—"

"Older?" Tanner finished.

Dusty laughed. "Well, that, too, but what I was going to say was that you've always had the ranch. You had something else besides rodeo. I haven't and don't. For me it's been bull riding and nothing else."

"This partnership would give you that," Tanner pointed out. "And then maybe you and Kate might— well, whatever you want. *If* you want, that is."

And in that moment, Dusty knew it was time to put Kate out of his mind and walk away. He'd never seriously considered leaving rodeo for her anyway, and it was his own fault she didn't want to see him anymore. Unfortunately, that didn't make it any easier for him to accept.

"She knows the score, Tanner," he told his friend. "I never let her think any different. I'm not that kind of man."

Tanner frowned. "I know you're not. Never thought you were. But I hoped—"

Dusty laughed, but it held no humor. "What? That I'd experience the same wedded bliss you have with Jules? Not likely. My track record with marriage isn't good."

"That was a long time ago," Tanner reminded him. "You were young."

"And I'm still young enough to follow my dream," Dusty said, determined to get on with the life he knew and loved.

"Even if it might cost you your life?"

"It's what I know. I wouldn't know how to be a good husband. I couldn't work at a job that kept me tied to a desk or even to a building. I love the danger riding bulls gives me, and the elevated danger will make it even more exciting."

Shaking his head, Tanner sighed. "I don't believe that last part. Not with what you know you have to deal with."

Dusty looked down at his hands, fisted on his thighs, and forced himself to flex his fingers. "Then you don't know me as well as I thought."

"Now wait just a minute," Tanner began. "Just because I don't agree with you and what you're doing with your life, that doesn't mean I won't support you and continue to value our friendship." A smile slowly appeared and he chuckled. "I can't promise Jules will feel the same way, though."

Dusty's laugh was sincere. "I doubt she will, but she'll forgive me."

Tanner's smile vanished. "Not if you get yourself killed."

"Then I guess I won't do that," Dusty said, getting to his feet. "And I need to get on my way."

"Are you planning to ride soon?" Tanner asked, as he followed Dusty to the door.

"I'm leaving early Saturday morning for Oregon. Rodeo starts on Wednesday."

Tanner opened the door for both of them. "You're driving?"

"It's the only way a cowboy should travel," Dusty said with a grin. He'd logged thousands of miles over his lifetime, and he'd enjoyed every minute of it.

"Alone? Isn't there some way—"

"No. There's no way."

"What—"

"She cut me loose, Tanner," Dusty finally admitted. "She doesn't want me around."

"Because you won't quit bull riding?"

Dusty shook his head, but then shrugged. "*Maybe.* That's probably part of it. I don't know for sure."

Jules came around the corner, frowning. "Maybe you should find out." Slipping her arm through Tanner's she gave Dusty a sad smile. "I know Kate doesn't have the same problem with you that I had with Tanner. But there are other issues—"

"If you hadn't told her—"

"What?" Jules asked. "What the doctor told you?" She glanced up at Tanner before going on. "We thought maybe you would listen to her."

"It doesn't concern her," Dusty said.

Jules stared at him, shaking her head. "It's no wonder she cut you loose then." Reaching out, she put her hand on his arm. "I'm sorry, Dusty. I shouldn't have said that. But think long and hard about what you're doing. Not only for Kate's sake, but for yours."

He nodded and gave her hand a friendly squeeze. "I have, and still do. If I think I'm not able to do my best, I'll quit." He remembered when he'd warned her to end it with Tanner if she couldn't be comfortable with his bronc riding, and it made him smile. "I guess that makes us even with advice and all."

Jules smiled. "Not at all. We consider you family, so we're free to give you all the advice we feel you need."

Dusty laughed, and a warmth settled around his heart. He couldn't ask for better friends. He took Tanner's hand and shook it, and then kissed Jules on the cheek. "I'll keep in touch."

"You'd better," Jules told him, "or we'll track you down. And don't think I'm kidding."

"Good luck, buddy," Tanner said.

As Dusty walked down the hall and out the front door, a part of him wished things could be different. But as he'd told Tanner, he was a rodeo cowboy. He'd been footloose and fancy-free all his adult life, doing whatever he wanted, when he wanted. And he'd liked it. He'd loved it. But then he met Kate, and in spite of believing he could walk away with no regrets, it wasn't happening. Nothing was the same since Kate. It had him all tied up in knots, and the only thing he knew to do about it was just keep on the way he had been, before they met. In less than a week, he'd be back riding bulls, and maybe then he'd feel at peace again.

KATE WIPED the sweat from her forehead and frowned. She hated driving this old tractor, but they'd had an offer for the good one with the cab, and if she wanted to get the edges of the fields worked up before the Fourth of July, the old tractor would have to do. None of them wanted to see a careless firework catch a field of wheat stubble on fire, but it happened every year. Working the edges would discourage a fire from starting, and if one started anyway, it could keep a runaway blaze from spreading more quickly to another field.

She stopped the tractor and climbed off to grab a jug of water she'd left at the edge of the field. Aggie and Trish had gone into Desperation, prompting Kate to do something, *anything,* to keep her mind off unpleasant memories. It didn't seem to be working, because the argument with Dusty the night before kept running through her mind.

None of them had heard from him after she'd told him to leave them all alone. She had been harsh and bordering on cruel, she knew, but at the time she'd felt like a wounded animal and had struck out in defense. When she'd gone home, licking her wounds, Aunt Aggie had noticed something was wrong, but hadn't asked any questions.

Kate just wanted to be left alone. She already missed Dusty, but she was too proud to apologize. Doing so wouldn't help the situation, only prolong it.

As she started to climb on the machine, she heard the sound of an approaching vehicle over the drone of the tractor. Shading her eyes with her hand, she turned to look. Her stomach turned a somersault when she saw Dusty's pickup turning into the drive. She watched as he stopped and climbed out, striding toward the edge of the field where she waited, too surprised to move.

"I want to talk to you," he shouted.

Her heart pounded and her hands shook as she forced herself to move and climbed onto the tractor, pretending she hadn't heard him. She needed to buy some time to get herself under control. She couldn't let him know that in less than a day she was already missing him.

"Get over here, Kate, or I'll have to drag you off that tractor," he bellowed as he started across the field toward her. "Come on, Kate. We need to talk."

Her gaze took in every inch of him. From his sandy brown hair to the scuffed toes of his boots, he looked wonderful. But she wasn't ready to face him yet.

Ignoring him, she shoved the tractor into gear and popped the clutch, lurching forward. Tears stung her eyes. If only she hadn't let her temper and her pride get the best of her. She could love him until the day she died, and she knew she probably would. But she couldn't take the risk of loving and losing him. It was better this way.

With her vision blurred by tears, she didn't notice how far she'd gone. She could see him running beside the tractor, shouting and waving his arms, and she still ignored him. It wasn't until she saw the far edge of the field coming up that she realized she was in trouble. Past it, the ground took a steep drop, ending several yards below in the creek. With the rain they'd had in the spring, and the recent thunderstorm, the water was deep. The last time she'd looked, only days before, it ran swiftly, the current racing.

Knowing she had little time to slow down to turn before she and the tractor would go over the edge, she slammed on the brakes. But the machine didn't even slow down. Panic rose in her throat. She looked at Dusty, who was desperately trying to keep up with her on foot, and she froze in terror. Even if the tractor survived the fall, she wouldn't.

"Stop the tractor!" she heard him shout. "Kate! Stop!"

"I can't!" she screamed.

"The brakes! Hit the brakes!"

The edge of the field was within sight, no more than fifty feet away. At the speed she was going, it would be only seconds before she and the tractor plunged into the creek.

"Kate! Jump!" she heard him yell.

Peeling her gaze from the edge, she saw him gaining on the tractor. "I can't!"

"Damn it, Kate. Jump!"

Without thinking, she leapt from the seat, blessedly avoiding the rotating rear tire, and crashed into him.

Chapter Eleven

Rolling with her, Dusty held tight, his arms locked around Kate as they tumbled away from the tractor and finally came to a stop. He watched as the machine rolled down the ravine into the creek. Beneath him, Kate lay still. He freed his arm from beneath her, and his hand shook as he brushed away the dirt and hair covering her face.

"We made it, hon. The tractor didn't, but we did," he told her with a weak laugh.

Kate didn't respond.

Dusty's chest closed on his next breath. "Kate, honey, please answer me."

She was so pale that the freckles across her nose and cheeks stood out like stars on a clear December night. Forcing himself to take a breath, he eased his other arm from beneath her and caressed her near-white cheek, urging her to open her eyes.

"Look at me, Kate. Open your eyes and look at me," he coaxed. When she still didn't respond, terror clogged his throat. Not knowing what else to do, he checked her pulse and found it beating, slowly and evenly. He then checked her arms and legs for broken bones. Finding none, he prayed it wasn't her neck or back. Or a concussion. He knew how dangerous that could be.

Even in his panic he knew she should have medical attention, and he reached for his cell phone in his pocket. It was gone. Somehow he had lost it, either while chasing through the field or rolling with her on the ground.

He could use the phone in the house, but he hated leaving her lying there alone, so he checked her one more time and found a small cut on the back of her arm. As he wiped the bit of warm, sticky blood from his fingers onto his jeans, she moved.

"Kate, I'm here, hon. Open your eyes."

"Dusty?" she whispered and moved as if trying to sit up.

"Be still," he told her.

"I'm all right," she said, struggling.

With his hands on her shoulders, he gently kept her from sitting. "Let's make sure you're okay first."

"Dusty, I'm—"

"Please," he begged, holding her in place. If anything was wrong with her— He refused to think about it, but only when she relented did he let go of her. "Do you hurt anywhere? Is there any pain?"

"No. I told you, I'm all right."

A frown drew her brows down, and he couldn't tell if it was from pain or from something else. "Move your right leg," he instructed.

"Oh, for the love of—"

"Kate," he cut her off, none too nicely. "Just this once, do what I say and don't argue with me."

With a sigh devoid of patience, Kate moved her leg.

"Now the other."

She moved it and grimaced with pain. "My ankle. I think I twisted it."

Dusty nodded. "Okay. We can deal with that. Now, move your arms, one at a time."

She did as he directed.

"Good. How's your head?"

Before he could stop her, she sat up in one quick motion and grabbed her head. "Ohhhh," she groaned.

Dusty grinned at her, but he was still shaken. "Yeah, that's what it's like."

She glanced at him, and then looked around. "Where's the tractor?"

"Having a bath," he answered as he carefully helped her to stand. Once she was on her feet, he scooped her into his arms.

"I can walk," she insisted.

"You can limp," he corrected.

"Then let me limp."

He looked down at her. "Nope. I'm going to take you up to the house. Are Aggie and Trish home?"

"They went to visit friends in the city."

"Aggie must have built-in radar," he said, chuckling.

"Meaning?"

"I wanted to spend some time with you," he explained. "Alone."

"Oh."

He'd come to tell her he was leaving soon, but it would wait until later, when he was sure she was okay. Until then, he would try to make her comfortable and hope there was nothing wrong with her that wouldn't easily and quickly heal.

They'd reached the porch without Dusty noticing

how far they'd come. She felt so good in his arms that he didn't think he could ever let her go. But that, he knew, wasn't going to happen.

"Maybe I should take you into town to see the doctor," he said, worried about the amount of time she'd been unconscious.

"I told you, I'm all right," she insisted. "Now, if you'll just put me down, I'll clean up and go check on the tractor."

"Can't," he said when they came to the door. Turning the knob, he shoved the door open with his shoulder and carried her through the kitchen and into the hall. "Where's your room?"

"My bedroom?" she asked.

There was something in her voice that made his blood race and his heart pound. Or maybe it was just hearing her say the word *bedroom*. Instead of answering, he nodded.

"Why?"

That stopped him in his tracks. It wasn't his intention to do anything more than make sure she was comfortable and wait for her family to return. But images of her lying on a bed, her coppery hair fanned out on a pillow, burst into his mind. It took every ounce of control he had to erase them so he could answer her.

"For one thing, you'll be more comfortable, and for another, you need to keep that foot elevated." She nodded her understanding, and he smiled, hoping it wasn't anything near leering. "Your bedroom is upstairs?" he asked, nodding toward the stairs.

"First door on the right."

Without hesitating, he carried her to the stairs and up

them to the room she'd indicated. Placing her on the bed, he turned.

"Are you leaving?" she asked, a hint of panic in her voice.

"I'm going to get some ice for your ankle," he explained.

"Dusty, my ankle will be fine. See?" She stood, placing her weight on both feet, and immediately moaned, as her knees buckled.

He caught her and held her. Even after her accident and roll in the plowed field, she still smelled like spring rain. He breathed deeply, closing his eyes and holding it in his memory. Her heart thudded against his chest, and her breathing quickened. Noticing how his own body responded from having her so close, he gently released her and sat her on the edge of the bed.

"Maybe we'd better get your boot off before it has to be cut off." Even he heard the husky quality in his voice. This wasn't the time. He looked up to smile, hoping she hadn't noticed, and she smiled in return, her gaze never leaving his. Kneeling on one knee in front of her, he pulled as gently as he could. By the look on her face, he could tell that even being gentle hurt her. "You need that ice," he said and moved to stand.

"Dusty?"

Looking up, he saw the indecision in her eyes.

"Why are you here?"

Unable to drag his gaze from hers, his mouth went dry and the words he had meant to say stuck in his throat. This wasn't how he'd planned it. He'd wanted to take her for a long drive until the sun began to set, find a quiet place to stop, turn on the radio to some soft music and tell her— He'd tell her he was leaving. Now it didn't seem like such a great idea.

"There's straw in your hair," he managed to say, reaching up to take it out. But the moment his hand brushed her cheek, he lost control. He moved closer until his lips met hers. He hadn't meant for it to happen, but it was impossible to stop, now that he'd started. She was in control now, not him.

KATE WAS STILL SHAKEN from her wild ride and the tumble from the tractor, but at the touch of Dusty's lips on hers, she knew she couldn't stop him. She didn't want to. It was crazy for her to want someone so badly when she knew it would lead her nowhere, but she couldn't stop. And it scared her.

Her fear soon evaporated in a mist of need as his gentle kiss changed to a passionate exploration. She wanted more, but she didn't know how to let him know. Even at twenty-six she admitted she was naive, but she was willing to learn. Very willing.

When he ended the kiss before she was ready for him to, she was afraid she had done something wrong. She searched his face for clues of what she might have done, but other than signs of a passion she was unfamiliar with, she saw nothing.

He moved away, lingering a brief moment to brush his fingers along her cheek. "I think I'd better get that ice, before your ankle swells even more."

"It'll be fine." She wished he would stay and kiss her again, but he was out the door before she could do anything.

And just how was she supposed to let him know that

she might be ready for one of the most important steps in her adult life? She *thought* she was ready, and if he'd only kiss her again, there was a strong possibility doubt would completely vanish.

Left alone to ponder the situation, she glanced around the room. Seeing it the way he might see it, she realized it hadn't grown up with her. It was still the room of a teenager, complete with a Desperation Dragons pennant on the wall and a bulletin board full of memorabilia. But she wasn't that shy teenaged girl any longer. She'd grown into a fairly confident young woman who owned a business and was well respected by most people. She just didn't know how to handle men.

Why couldn't she be more like her sister when it came to the opposite sex? Trish had never had a problem. Men had always flocked to her, but no one had seemed to be the one she wanted until the day Morgan had stopped them for not coming to a complete stop at a stop sign. She didn't have any idea if Trish had been interested in him before that, but from that day on, there was no doubt that Trish believed Sheriff Morgan Rule was *the one*. Being the younger of the two, she had asked Trish how she knew what to say and do, and Trish had told her she simply trusted her instincts. Kate had snorted at the advice, saying she didn't believe she'd been born with any, at least when it came to men.

Trust your instincts.

She could try….

When she heard footsteps start up the stairs, panic hit her. Dusty had liked her in her dress at the Blue Barn, and he'd liked her hair down. She certainly didn't have time to change into a dress or anything remotely similar, but she did have time to do something with her hair. Tugging off the elastic band that held what was left of her braid, she ran her fingers through the plaits to separate them. She could hear his footsteps in the hall and managed to grab a brush from the bedside table, run it through her hair once, toss it back in the drawer and hopefully look enticing…if that was possible.

"We probably should try getting that boot—" Dusty stopped in the doorway and stared. "Kate."

"Hmm?"

He shook his head. "Nothing." Moving again, he stopped at the side of her bed. "Your boot?"

"Yes, let's try again," Kate agreed.

He set the bag of ice on the floor and bent over, taking the heel of her boot in his hand. "Let me know if it hurts too much."

She concentrated on his head as he wiggled the boot on her foot. His light brown hair was still in need of a haircut and curled at the ends. Her fingers itched to touch it, but she wasn't sure—

Trust your instincts.

Reaching out, she touched his temples and ran her fingers gently back through his hair. He gave a strangling sound and stopped moving the boot. "Are you all right?" she asked.

He cleared his throat but didn't look up at her. "Yes. I think I'm about there." His head jerked up and he stared at her for an instant, then he lowered his head just as quickly. "I mean, I think I've about got the boot off."

Kate smiled. Maybe she'd been born with instincts

after all. Before she could try anything else, the boot came off her foot. "Ouch!"

Off balance and with boot in hand, Dusty hit the floor. "Sorry," he said. He grabbed the bag of ice and got to his feet. "Can you swing your legs onto the bed?"

Could she? Leaning back on her hands, she was able to move one leg to the bed, but when she tried the other, her ankle screamed in pain. Biting her lip, she shook her head.

"Then I'll do it for you." Touching her leg as if it were made of glass, he gently moved it onto the bed and placed the ice bag over her swollen ankle. "Better?"

She turned her head to answer him and stared right at the area below his large belt buckle. *Oh, my.* Had she caused that? Slowly raising her gaze, she stopped at his face and understood what the phrase "smoldering eyes" meant.

Trust your instincts.

"Dusty?" she whispered.

He leaned down, closer. "What do you need, Kate? What can I do?"

He'd asked the perfect questions, and she knew she'd be a fool not to answer them honestly. Without speaking, she slipped her arms around his neck. She didn't know how she knew to do it, but she pulled him down onto the bed with her. His lips touched her throat, his mouth blazing a trail of tastes and nibbles.

She tugged at his shirt, pulling it up his body. He moved enough so she could slip it over his head, and then she tossed the shirt aside. Staring at his tanned, muscled chest, all inhibitions vanished, and her instincts took over completely. This time, it was the buttons on her own shirt she attacked, but Dusty brushed her hands aside. As the buttons came undone, his lips followed, and he slipped the edges of the fabric apart.

Kate gasped when he cupped one breast and kissed through the filmy fabric of her bra. Thinking was impossible as need took over, but there was no need to think as together they finished the job and tossed their clothes to the floor.

Easing onto the bed to lie beside her, he stroked her cheek with his knuckles. "Now's the time to say stop." His voice was husky and dark like his eyes. "I can't promise anything after this."

Shaking her head, her gaze never left his. "If I didn't want this, it wouldn't be happening."

With a low, rumbling groan, he pulled her on top of him, his hands touching and caressing her as his deep kiss possessed her. She pressed herself to him, instinct moving her hips in a slow rotation.

When he smoothly rolled her to move her beneath him, she moaned his name. His mouth traveled every inch of her and more until she thought she would die with wanting. She lifted her hips, silently begging for what they both craved. Parting her legs, she felt him move to press against her. Their gazes fused as he slowly entered her, inch by agonizing inch.

Her breath caught when he stopped, his eyes widening.

"No," he sighed, the disbelief in his eyes clear.

When he started to move away, she held him with one word. "Please," she begged.

His eyes closed and his body tensed beneath her hands. "No, we'll wait," he said.

"Now," she pleaded. "I wanted it to be right."

"We can wait—"

She didn't let him finish as she lifted her hips, drawing him deeper. "It's right," she gasped.

"Don't do this to me," he groaned.

She gave him no choice when she wrapped her legs around him, driving him deeper.

"Be still," he told her when she started to move. "Let me."

She felt the first wave hit her, sending her free-falling into a word of colors. Tumbling, she floated in a world of sensations until he cried out her name.

Their bodies wrapped around each other and their hearts slowed to a steady rhythm, bringing a smile to Kate's lips as she sighed with pleasure. Dusty raised his head to look at her, his eyes still smoky. A smile eased the angles of his face as he pressed his hand to her cheek.

"See what happens?" he asked. "See what you do to me? I completely forgot what I came to tell you."

She turned her head to press a kiss to his palm. "What's that?"

"I'll be leaving in a few days, and—"

"Back to riding bulls?" A chill of fear shot through her. She had known it was coming, sooner or later, but she'd held out hope that he might suddenly have some common sense when it came to his life.

"That's what I do."

She couldn't continue to be silent about it. "Even though it could mean serious injury? Or maybe even death? I know what the doctor said. I know what numerous concussions can cause."

"That's the decision I've made."

"Why?"

He shrugged one shoulder. "Why not? Rodeo has been my life since I was seventeen. It's what I know best, and I'm good at it. I'd be a fool to walk away from it."

The stubborn determination in his eyes almost made her give up, but she couldn't. "Rodeo could *end* your life, too," she reminded him.

"That's a risk I'm willing to take," he said, avoiding eye contact. Tugging at her disheveled hair, he twisted a strand of it around his finger. When he looked directly at her, his eyes were soft and needful. "Come with me, Kate."

Disappointment warred with a short burst of happiness. "I can't, Dusty."

"Why not? With Aggie leasing the farmland, how will you keep busy?"

Trish had been told, and Aggie had let people know her plan. A few had professed interest, but Kate wasn't ready to give up yet. "I have my accounting. Besides, this is home."

"How do you know? You've never really seen anything else. Come with me and see the sights. Maybe you'll find a place you like even more."

All she could do was look at him, still unable to understand what drove him to do what he did. Apparently he felt the same about her. "You really don't understand, do you? Home means nothing to you."

"Maybe someday it will."

"If that's what you believe, it never will. So go. There's nothing keeping you here." It was time to let go. She had no hold on him and never would.

"I'll be back," he told her, as if it would change things. "I'll come back to see you, if that's what you're wondering."

She couldn't look at him. "Why should it matter?"

"Because it does. At least to me." He paused for a moment, but she didn't allow herself to hope. "I don't know what the future will bring, but I grew up knowing that rodeo and marriage don't work. I even tried it myself and learned the hard way."

"Who said I was interested in marriage?" she asked, battling for her pride. "I don't need you or anyone else. I know what I want out of life. I have plans for the future. Goals. You don't, and that's where we part ways. Don't worry about those feelings you might have. I'm sure they're nothing. And don't bother about coming back to see me. It isn't necessary."

He shook his head, rolling away from her and leaving the bed to sit on the edge of it. "You remind me of my mother. She was just as stubborn as you are, and for most of my life I didn't like her."

She felt the cold of his absence, but refused to let him see it affected her. "If that's your way of giving someone a compliment—"

"Now that I've met you, I'm beginning to understand her more. She worked hard to keep a roof over our heads when my dad left. When she remarried, I hated the man, but now I see that he's not the villain I thought he was. In fact, he's a pretty good guy."

It wasn't as easy as she thought it would be to remain unemotional and uninvolved. "Do you see them often?"

"I don't see them at all. They live in Arizona now. She keeps trying though, and calls me once or twice a year."

Turning her head so she wouldn't have to look in his

eyes, she kept all emotion from her voice. "Maybe you should call *her* and tell her that you appreciate what she did for you."

"Yeah. Maybe." But he didn't seem convinced.

She felt him hesitate, and then lean on the bed. Reaching out, he caught the end of her hair and trailed it across her breasts. The bed shifted before his lips found what he'd just teased, and she hated that she couldn't stop the way her body responded. She was his, body, heart and soul.

And he planned to leave.

"Maybe I should check on that tractor," she said, moving away from him.

He caught her and pulled her closer to trail kisses over her throat. "You're not going anywhere," he murmured, before he pressed his lips to hers and entered her again.

Kate groaned at the intense pleasure he gave her. Had she been foolish enough to believe that if they made love, everything would fall into place? She didn't think so.

Later, when he was gone, she lay on her bed in the silent house wondering when regret would set in. When it didn't, she went over every moment they'd been together, gathering memories to last the rest of her life. Had Aunt Aggie done the same?

Now she had even more reason to never marry. No other man would be able to take Dusty's place in her heart. If he ever returned to Desperation—and she doubted he would—he could never know how much she loved him. She couldn't risk that. In a tiny corner of her heart, there would always be the fear that she would lose him, just as she had her parents. Letting him go now would be easier than losing him later.

She would always keep these moments close in her heart. He would just never know it.

Chapter Twelve

Dusty spent the night and all the next day wishing he had done things differently. He hadn't meant to let things go so far, but he'd been hard pressed to refuse Kate. He wanted to tell her he was sorry he hadn't been the gentleman he'd always believed he was. He wanted to tell her a lot of things. But all he could tell her was goodbye.

With a feeling of heaviness in his heart, he knocked on the Claybornes' door. When Aggie answered, he tried to state his intentions in a calm, clear manner.

"I need to talk to Kate."

"She's not here, Dusty," Aggie answered, propped against the door.

Disappointed to the point of desperation, Dusty pulled off his hat and swore under his breath. He looked at Aggie. "Can I come in and wait?"

Hesitating at first, Aggie smiled and held the door open. "Might as well. I'm here all alone," she said as she sat in her chair at the table. "Trish is visiting Hettie for the night. Kate was supposed to give her some cooking lessons today, but Hettie offered to do it. Trish is getting better at it, but I pity poor Morgan. Of course you don't have to worry about anything like that."

Dusty tried for a smile. He wasn't sure what to do or say. He hadn't planned on a conversation with Aggie about her niece's cooking skills.

"Don't just stand there," Aggie told him with a wave of her hand. "Pull up a chair. You're gonna have a long wait."

Before his butt hit the chair, Dusty stopped and looked at her. "Why?"

Aggie took a long drink of her ever-present coffee while he continued to sit. "She's at the Blue Barn."

Dusty felt his blood run cold. Narrowing his eyes, he stared at her. "What's she doing there?"

Shrugging, Aggie avoided his gaze. "Oh, whatever it is that people do at the Blue Barn. Personally, I've never stepped inside the place, but folks don't see things the way I do."

"She ought to know better than to go there alone again," he grumbled.

Aggie cleared her throat and looked at him, a nervous tick causing her right eye to twitch. "She didn't go alone."

Dusty's heartbeat thundered in his ears. "Who's she with?"

"Well, now, Dusty," she hedged, "I don't know that I ought to tell you that. I don't know that it's any of your business."

The edges of the room began to turn red. "I'm making it my business."

"I don't know what you did to my poor Kate," Aggie said, a mournful frown on her face, "but that girl was just *moping* around this place all day."

"She was?" He wasn't sure exactly what that meant, but it definitely meant something.

"Well, that and biting everybody's head off," she added.

He noticed the twinkle of mischief in her eyes. Realizing what she was up to, he leaned back in his chair and tipped his hat down over his eyes. He hadn't missed Aggie's attempts at matchmaking and, at times, had been grateful. But tonight she wanted him riled up and crazy. She counted on him to run off half-cocked to drag Kate out of the Blue Barn. Well, he wouldn't give either of them the satisfaction.

"I reckon I'll just hang around until she wanders on home," he said, hiding his smile. "You got any more of that coffee? Could be a long night."

He heard and felt the smack on the table. "Dusty McPherson, you're a bigger fool than I thought," she declared.

Although the sound of her hand hitting the table had jarred him, he attempted to play it cool. Tipping his hat back with a knuckle, he smiled at her. "Now, Miss Aggie—"

"Get your good lookin' butt out of here and go get her," she demanded in a way only Miss Aggie could. "If you care anything at all about her, you'll grab her by the hair and haul her out of there, before she gets into trouble."

"If she's with somebody she should be safe, even at the Blue Barn," he assured her.

"Depends on who she's with, doesn't it?"

He waited as the air thickened in the suddenly silent kitchen, while Aggie looked at him. He didn't want to make a guess.

"Who's she with?" he finally asked.

When she told him, Dusty let out a string of swear words on his way to the door and hit the ground outside at a run.

ADJUSTING HIS EYES to the dim interior of the Blue Barn, Dusty cringed at the loud music that assaulted him as he searched for Kate. The place was packed with people, but he didn't see any of them. He was busy searching for only one particular redhead as he pushed his way through to the dance floor. After a quick look around, he started to turn to find a better spot, but a flash of auburn caught his attention.

He had calmed down since he'd left Aggie at the farm, until he saw Kate on the dance floor in the arms of the last man Dusty wanted to see her with. Just as Miss Aggie had told him, Ted Haverly had his arms wrapped around her. Dusty felt the cavernous room shrink as everything in his view disappeared except her. Setting his jaw, his fists clenched in tight balls, he made his way to the dancing couple, not caring who he ran over to get there. Unable to speak, he reached them and wrapped his fingers around Kate's upper arm.

"Hey, Dusty," Ted protested. "The lady is with me."

Dusty slid his glare to the man. "You only got one part of that right, Haverly. The *lady* part." He tugged on Kate as she tried to pry his hand off. One look in her eyes told him he was pushing his luck with her. Whether Kate was agreeable to a dance or not didn't matter. Letting go of her arm, he managed to pull her into his arms, ignoring her partner.

Ted attempted to put himself between them. "Seems

to me you could use some lessons on how to treat a lady," he suggested, a mean glint in his eyes.

Dusty forced a smile. With an effort, he pushed down the insult he wanted to say and reminded himself he never cared much for fighting. But he'd never had jealousy push at him before, either, and he couldn't say he liked it all that much.

"This won't take long, Ted," Kate said, with a warning look for Dusty. Ted walked away with a shrug and no comment. Kate's eyes blazed when she looked up at Dusty. "I've never known you to be rude and nasty."

Dusty squeezed his eyes shut and swallowed the misery she was putting him through. "I can't help it," he admitted. "Just the thought of him—" He shook his head, trying to get the picture of them together out of his mind.

"It's none of your business what I do," she snapped. "You don't have any right—"

"Don't I?" he asked, locking his gaze with her fiery one. He felt her hands resting on his chest, sure she would push him away any second. Fine. He'd just push first, in his own way. "Seems to me you've got that a little wrong," he went on, shoving his luck a little further.

The muted lights cast strange shadows across her face, but even in the dark, it glowed with a blush. "You're wrong."

He shook his head, holding her tighter. "You asked me to, hon. I remember you distinctly—"

She had spun around and was gone before he knew what was happening. Being bigger, he was able to get through the crowd with sheer size and followed her. He reached the door as it swung shut behind her.

The parking lot fluorescents afforded him little light to see much, but luckily his hearing was better than average, and he knew where she was.

"Damn it, Kate," he swore, "just listen to me."

"Don't you dare touch me," she whispered from the shadows of the building. "I was having a good time before you showed up acting like a...a..."

"Jealous fool?" he asked, sneaking up to capture her in the dark.

"That's close," she sniffed.

"It's your fault," he whispered.

When she twisted in his arms, he pressed his body against hers to hold her still. "If you don't stop fighting, I'm going to take you home," he warned her. "And don't think I won't." She settled down again, and he breathed a sigh of relief. "Now maybe we can talk."

"We have nothing to talk about."

"Oh, yes, we do." He held her stubborn gaze with his own.

She closed her eyes, breaking the contact, and sighed. Opening them, she relented. "What do you want, Dusty?"

Now that she was giving him the chance, he wasn't sure exactly how to say it, so he said all he could. "I came to say goodbye."

A flash of sadness crossed her face, but disappeared immediately, replaced by a stubborn tilt to her chin. "I thought we already did that. Yesterday."

He knew he'd bungled it, but he hadn't realized how badly. "Yesterday had nothing to do with it, except that I was going to tell you then. I couldn't say it though. And I couldn't leave without seeing you again. I don't know how long I'll be gone, but—" He hadn't expected her to run off to the Blue Barn at the first opportunity. And he sure hadn't expected her to be there with another man. "Just tell me one thing, Kate."

She wouldn't look at him. "What's that?"

"What are you doing *here?*"

"I'm doing what you suggested. I'm getting some perspective."

Frustrated, he shook his head. "You know this isn't what I meant."

"It isn't?" Her smile was small and tight, a definite sign of her belligerence.

"Kate, don't sell yourself short. You're better than this."

"And what's wrong with this?" She gestured toward the building behind them. "It's not all that different than the life you lead. A lot of these people are like you. Live for the moment, travel from one place to another and to another—"

"No, it's not the same," he said, shaking his head. "My life is…well, okay. My life may be similar in that respect, and it *is* different than yours. But that's no reason—"

"My point, exactly."

He didn't know what he could say to change things back. He couldn't believe that what had happened the day before could have changed her so much. "I won't ride bulls forever, you know."

"And then what?"

He shook his head. He'd never given a lot of thought to what he would do when that day came, or even if it would come. That's not how he had lived.

"Or what if something happens to you?" she continued. "Next week? Next month?"

"It won't." He wouldn't let it.

She was watching him, watching his face so closely he could almost feel her gaze penetrate deep into his mind. "You're pretty confident, aren't you?" she asked.

He needed to make her understand. "I have to be to do what I do. Otherwise, I would've been stomped flat a long time ago." He'd even come close to that happening, more than once, but it hadn't kept him from climbing back on a bull and doing it all over again. "Besides, if something does happen, it isn't going to affect anyone but me."

Again, there was a flash of sadness in her eyes, and this time it remained. "You really believe that, don't you?"

"I've made sure it's that way."

"It's your life," she said, her voice flat and unemotional and not at all like her. "And if nothing happens and you keep riding, that's good. I hope it goes that way. But that isn't what this is about."

"Then what is?"

He watched as she seemed to struggle with whatever it was she wanted to say. Finally, she looked him square in the eye.

"You can't commit, Dusty. Not to people. Not to one person. Not even to yourself. You take responsibility for yourself only, and you don't do a great job of that. No aspirations, no plans beyond rodeo. When you're too old to do that, you don't know what you'll do, because you can't look beyond the moment. I don't know why. Maybe you do."

Her words made him uncomfortable and he shrugged his shoulders. "I don't see the need to."

She stepped back and he let her. "And I don't see the need to continue this conversation. I'd like to get back to my date. Goodbye, Dusty," she said with a sad smile. "Good luck on the rodeo circuit. And I really do mean that."

He couldn't let her walk away. "I'll come back, you know. Someday." But he didn't know when.

"If you do, please don't bother to stop by."

Reaching out before she could get away, he took her hand. "This isn't over. *We* aren't over."

"Yes, we are. We never really got started."

"What do you call yesterday? What do you call this?" He pulled her to him and captured her lips with his. She didn't struggle or fight him, but he could tell her heart wasn't in it.

When he released her, she took a step back. "I call it lust."

He felt as if he'd been slapped. "It's more than lust, Kate. I have feelings for you, real feelings, but I don't know yet what they are or what to do about them."

"You'll forget about me in no time," she said, unable to meet his gaze, "and I'll eventually forget about you. But I can't promise I won't worry about you, at least for a little while."

There was nothing else he could say. Releasing her, he forced air into his lungs. Not that it mattered. At that moment, he didn't care if he remembered to take another breath.

Stepping away, Kate smoothed the skirt of her clingy dress. Without looking back, she opened the heavy door of the Blue Barn.

"Kate," he called after her. "Kate!"

But she didn't turn around before she walked inside. Dusty would have given up if he hadn't heard the hitch in her breath when she had walked away. No matter what she said, Kate cared, and he'd carry that with him forever.

DUSTY PUT the nineteen-hundred-mile drive across six states to good use by getting his head on straight. By the time he arrived in Woodburn, Oregon, he was ready to ride, not only physically, but mentally. He'd left Desperation and Oklahoma and even Kate behind. He was back doing what he did best, and he was happy to be there.

He chose to stay in the host hotel, something he didn't usually do, but he had a reason to celebrate. He'd been away from the circuit for too long and needed to be in the thick of things. He was ready. Adrenaline had already started pumping through him.

After his arrival the evening before, he'd spent several hours with cowboys he hadn't seen since his accident, catching up on the news he'd missed. After sleeping in an extra hour that morning, he'd spent some time in the fitness area, making sure he had the strength he'd need to climb on a bull, and then he had a swim in the pool.

Before leaving for the arena, he thought to stop at the reception desk to check for any messages.

"There's one message, sir," the young woman behind the desk told him with a smile.

Taking the note she passed him, he opened it and read the short good-luck message from Tanner and Jules. He wouldn't allow himself to acknowledge there was nothing from Kate or anyone else. He didn't expect there to be. Things were back to normal.

The drive to the arena was short, and after parking his truck and retrieving his equipment bag, he checked in and picked up his number. He was fifth in the lineup, which was a bit of a disappointment, but he reminded himself that being out of competition for two months had dropped him in the standings. He'd make it up fast.

He was standing at the fence not far from the chute, watching the first of the rides for the night, when he caught a flash of auburn out of the corner of his eye. *Of course it isn't Kate,* he told himself, but it didn't keep his heart from hoping and hammering. Unable to stop, he walked in the direction where he'd seen the redhead, finally catching up with her. But when he touched her arm and she turned to face him, the disappointment was almost painful.

"Fool," he muttered to himself as he walked slowly back to the spot he'd come from. He listened to the announcement on the loudspeaker for the name of the next rider. Two more after that, and it would be his turn to prove himself. He needed to get ready for his ride.

But he couldn't.

Every conversation he'd had with Kate played through his mind. He wished they wouldn't. He had never had any intention of getting involved with someone. He'd seen what had happened with his parents, and he wouldn't repeat it. His mother had only wanted a family, but his father had wanted rodeo.

His doctor's prognosis echoed in his mind. *Worst-case scenario, death. But there are others, not quite so...final.*

Why had he thought he would be immune to any of the things his doctor had listed? He was human. And if something did happen to him, why did he think it wouldn't make a difference?

The next rider finished with a good score, and Dusty watched the cowboy limp out of the arena—just another man either dealing with an old injury or a new one. Injuries happened all the time.

Letting go of his stubborn determination to keep on as he always had, he thought about what life might be like outside of rodeo or at least outside of riding bulls for a living. Even Tanner had decided there were other things in life. And Dusty had always admired his friend.

And then the image of Kate's face floated in front of him, and he knew he had to make a change. Right or wrong, he needed to go in a new and different direction.

After checking out at the rodeo office and returning his number, he headed for his truck. He stopped for an instant to pull out his new cell phone and punched in a number he'd never used but had also never forgotten.

"Hi, Mom. It's Dusty," he said, when Tess Braden answered.

"Dusty? Oh, my goodness! Are you all right? Is something wrong?"

He chuckled, imagining the surprise on her face. "Yeah, it's me. I'm fine and nothing's wrong. I just wanted to call you."

There was a slight pause before she spoke again. "I'm glad you did, but I have to admit it's a surprise."

"I figured it would be. How's Frank?"

"He's good," she said. "He's out on the golf course right now."

Dusty tried to imagine an older version of his stepfather, a man he had never allowed himself to like. "So he's a golfer, huh? That fits and it's good that he stays active."

"Dusty, I know things were bad when you were young—"

He wouldn't let her finish. "Mom, you deserve a good man. My dad wasn't a good father, and he wasn't a good husband. I finally understand that."

"I'm sorry then, because you idolized him."

To deny it would have been a lie, so he didn't. "I need to tell you something else," he said, choosing his words carefully.

"What's that?"

Dusty felt a smile tug at his lips. "Thank you."

"Why, whatever for?"

"Everything," he told her, thinking back to when he was a boy. "All the sacrifices you made. The two jobs you worked and how you wanted me to make something of myself. For letting me go live with Granddad and Gramma. For teaching me right from wrong."

"Dusty, I—I don't know what to say."

He grinned, even knowing she couldn't see him. "Good. Because there isn't anything you should say. And I'm sorry I haven't been a better son."

"It's all right," she said, and he could hear the tears in her voice. "I understand. I know it wasn't easy for you either."

He hadn't called her to make her cry, only to let her know he was thinking of her and to tell her his news. "I've found somebody. Somebody special."

"That's wonderful, Dusty."

He could hear the smile in her voice and almost see her. "I think you'll like her. She's a lot like you."

"Like me?"

"Yeah, she's stubborn and hardworking and passionate about things. She knows what she wants to do with her life, and she'll get it. I know she will."

"She does sound special, but I don't think that sounds like me. Except maybe the stubborn part."

Her laughter made him smile, and for the first time since he was a young boy, he wished he could be with her. "I just quit rodeo, Mom. No more bull riding."

There was silence, and he wondered if it was too much, but she finally spoke again. "If I say I'm sorry," she said, "I'd be lying. It's a rough life, Dusty, as I'm sure you know. But it's what you wanted, and I never wanted anything more for you than to let you grow up and chase your dreams."

"I know that now. It took me a long time to figure it out. I guess I'm just hardheaded."

"Like me."

"Yeah, like you." The thought brought him happiness. "Could we come out sometime and visit you and Frank?"

"We'd love it if you did. Both of you. What's her name?"

"Kate. Kate Clayborne."

"Clayborne? That's familiar. Any relation to—"

"Agatha Clayborne's niece. Miss Aggie finished raising her and her sister when their parents died in a tornado."

"How awful for them. But if she was raised by Aggie Clayborne, I'm sure she has a good heart. Are you in Desperation?"

"Not right now, but I'm headed there. And maybe you and Frank can come visit us, too."

"For any special occasion?"

He knew she was angling for more, but he couldn't

tell her anything he didn't know. "Maybe. But I'll have to do some talking to get her to agree to that occasion."

"That shouldn't be hard. You've always been a charmer, even when you were a little boy."

He thought of how Kate had said she never wanted to see him again. "I have a feeling it's going to take more than charm to get her to see things my way."

"If she's that special, then you do whatever you have to."

"I will," he promised. "You can count on it. But I'd better say goodbye. I need to get on the road. I'll call you again. Soon."

"I don't know of anything I'd like better than that, Dusty. And let me know how things go with Kate. I'll keep my fingers crossed for you."

"Thanks, Mom. I need all the luck I can get."

"I love you, Dusty."

He felt his own eyes fill with emotion. "And I love you, too, Mom, even though it seemed for a long time that I didn't."

"Now is what counts."

He finished the call feeling better than he ever had. For him and his mother, the past hurts were put to rest. The future was ahead of him. He hoped Kate would be a part of that future, but there was only one way to find out if she would—if she'd even listen to him. Somehow, no matter what it took, he'd find a way.

Chapter Thirteen

Red, white and blue banners, strung across Main Street from light pole to light pole, waved in the breeze. Booths and tables stretched from one end of the main street of town to the other. Firecrackers popped in the distance. Desperation's annual Fourth of July celebration was in full swing, as hundreds of people wandered the streets, greeting friends, buying souvenirs and tasting food.

Kate, along with Aggie and Trish, was busy at their food booth, where they were serving tiny wedges of pie and selling and taking orders for full-sized ones. Several people had even urged her to start a catering business, and Kate was seriously giving it some thought—with help from her aunt and sister. To her, it was secretly a compromise to Dusty's restaurant suggestion. With a catering business, she could work as much or as little as she chose.

Taking the money from Mabel Schwimmer, Kate handed her the change and two pies. "I hope you like the peach. They're all made from fresh fruit."

"Oh, I know I will," Mrs. Schwimmer said. "I've

been eating them for years at the café. There's nothing better than your pies."

Kate thanked her, stowed the money away and then turned to help the next customer...and froze. "Wh-what are you doing here? I thought you were in Oregon."

"We need to talk."

Kate's heart thundered in her chest, but she tried to keep her voice steady and firm. "I'm busy right now, Dusty. Maybe later."

"No, not later. Now," he said, without skipping a beat.

Kate shook her head, realizing he knew her too well and wouldn't give her a chance to argue. Instead of answering him, which she knew would do nothing to end whatever conversation he wanted to have, she turned to a waiting customer. "What can I get you, Cathy?"

"Kate," he said, trying to claim her attention.

"There's the usual that you find every day at the Chick-a-Lick. Cherry, apple, peach and pecan. Or if you want to try a new one, we have some meringues."

But Dusty kept on. "I can wait all day, if that's the way you want to be."

When the customer had made a selection, paid, and was gone, Kate turned to address the irritation. "Go away, Dusty. Go ride a bull or rope a steer or something. Just go away."

She first thought he was doing as she wished, until she realized he was walking around to the opening between the tables at the back of their booth. Searching for another means of escape and finding none, she turned back again to find he had been swallowed up by the crowd. She couldn't see him anywhere.

Feeling somewhat safe, she returned to her spot and

straightened the many plates of pies, moving them around for a more pleasant presentation. When she felt a tug on her arm, she jumped, certain it was Dusty sneaking up on her. But instead, it was Aggie.

"Trish, help Mr. Murdock there for a minute, will you?" Aggie called over her shoulder. She led Kate to the far corner of the group of tables. "You've always been a stubborn miss," she said, keeping her voice low.

Kate saw trouble and hoped to avoid it. She didn't want to argue with her aunt anymore, but it seemed like that was all they'd been doing. "And lately you've been trying to get rid of me. Why?"

"I want to know that you're taken care of."

Not again, Kate thought. They'd been over this constantly since Dusty had left town. "I appreciate your concern, as always, Aunt Aggie, but I can take care of myself."

Aggie shook her head and released her. "I thought the same, too, but it can be lonely. I don't want that for you."

"I'll be fine." The look in Aggie's eyes made Kate want to cry. But if she did, Aggie would know how much she was hurting, and she couldn't stand anyone knowing that. And she *would* be fine, in time. The lease for the farmland was to be signed by a neighbor on Monday, but Kate was determined that someday she would get it back.

Aggie peered at her over a new pair of glasses. "It could be better. You know it could."

Kate held her ground. "No, I don't."

"Don't let this chance go by you, Kate," Aggie said, putting her hand on Kate's shoulder. "Grab what you can *when* you can, or someday you'll wish you'd done it different."

Kate hoped that someday her aunt would share the story of her lost love with her, but she doubted she ever would. And she really, really didn't want to talk about Dusty or her future. She hadn't meant to fall in love with him, but it had happened anyway. When she couldn't stop him from risking his life, she had told him goodbye, no matter how much it had hurt. Seeing him again was almost more than she could bear.

Looking around to make sure he wasn't anywhere in sight, she edged toward the gap in the tables.

"It won't help to run away," Aggie told her.

"I'm not running," Kate answered, but she stepped backward to where she knew she could get away if she needed to. "I just don't want—"

"Me?"

Kate spun around to find Dusty blocking her escape, a rope slung over his shoulder. Planting her hands on her hips, she glared at him. "You don't give up, do you?"

"Nope."

Knowing nothing he could say would change her mind, she shook her head. "I don't have time for games, Dusty."

Hooking his thumbs in his belt, he rocked back on his heels. "No games, but I think you should know that I don't plan to leave until you hear what I have to say."

"Then you'd better talk fast."

His smile was forced. "Hot date?"

"Customers to serve." She took a deep breath and stuffed her hands in her back pockets. "So if you have something to say, get it said."

His eyes narrowed, but his gaze never left her face. "You still seeing Ted Haverly?"

"That's none of your business."

His frown deepened. "Considering, I don't think the question is out of line."

She looked down to avoid the intensity of his gaze, and stared at the ground. She didn't want him to think he had any sort of chance, but she couldn't lie, either. "No, I'm not seeing Ted."

"You seeing anybody else?"

"You've been gone a week. What do you think?"

"You don't want to know what I think, so just answer the question."

She knew there were a number of ways he could find out if he wanted to, but he trusted her to tell him the truth. For some reason, she couldn't disappoint him. "No."

He bowed his head, but she didn't miss his smile, even though he tried to hide it. She wasn't sure whether to smack him or laugh with joy. The latter bothered her much more than the former.

He moved to step around the end of the table that separated them. "Well, I guess that takes care of that problem."

She took a step backward. "You can stop where you are."

Grinning, he kept moving. "There's no shotgun in your hand this time, hon."

Like a bolt of lightning, she shot around him, escaping the enclosure of the tables and him. Looking back over her shoulder, she saw that he was following her. And none too slowly. Picking up speed, she dashed into the crowd, hoping she could get lost in the throng of people moving along the main street.

She kept telling herself that he wasn't what she wanted. He never would be. When she noticed the open door of the café, she ducked inside, praying he'd lost sight of her, as her heart pounded in her chest.

"YOU CAN'T RUN FOREVER, Kate," Dusty called after her, as he slipped the rope from his shoulder. To his surprise and pleasure, the people in front of him parted, giving him a clear view as Kate came flying out of the café, with a surprised but troubled expression. Darla, the waitress at the café, stepped out of the doorway, shaking her head. It seemed she wasn't going to help Kate out of her predicament, and Dusty couldn't have been happier.

He lengthened his stride and watched as she hesitated, looking right and left, and he knew the moment she saw him. Unfortunately for her, the crowd was enjoying the show as she tried to zigzag her way through them.

He gained on her quickly, thanks to folks stepping aside for him. When he knew he was close enough and nobody would be in the way, he weighted the loop of his rope and tossed it at her. It slipped easily over her shoulders before he tugged it tight.

"What the—" She staggered as the breath whooshed out of her, but she stayed on her feet. He didn't want her hurt, just stopped, and he handled the rope with expert hands.

She looked around, as if she thought someone would step in to help her, but no one did. "Sheriff Rule," she shouted at the man who stood at the front of the crowd now surrounding them. "Do something, for heaven's sake. Stop him."

Morgan shook his head. "Can't do that, Kate. Looks to me like Dusty is just practicing his roping. No law against that."

Dusty smiled at the sheriff and nodded his thanks. Being careful not to hurt her, he began to haul Kate in. With each easy tug, he spoke. "You are—without a doubt—the most—stubborn—muleheaded—argumentative—independent—hot-tempered woman—I've ever known." He brought her to a halt in front of him, her arms held snugly at her sides by the rope.

"And I love you," he finished.

Unable to move, Kate's fury vanished. Her eyes stung and her lip trembled as she tried to speak. "This isn't fair," she whispered with a sniff.

"You haven't played fair, either," he pointed out. "You keep running off, instead of talking to me." Dropping the end of the rope, he caught it under his foot before taking her in his arms. He felt her tremble as he reached for her braid and slipped off the cord that bound the end. "You know I'm not one to give up, but this is the only time I'm going to ask you this," he said, sliding the twisted hair apart.

"Ask me what?"

He could feel the pounding of her heart beneath his chest. The crowd around them was silent, as if holding its breath to see what would happen next. He looked into her blue eyes and offered a silent prayer. "Kate Clayborne, will you marry me?"

When she shook her head, he heard the disappointment ripple through the crowd and felt the pain her refusal caused. But he wasn't going to walk away. Not yet. Maybe not ever.

Turning to the crowd, he kept a tight hold on Kate. "I know y'all want to know how this is going to turn out, and I can promise you won't be disappointed. But

Kate and I need some privacy to talk this over, so if you don't mind…"

With a collective groan, a few started to move away and others followed, pieces of their conversations drifting back to Dusty. He looked around for a quiet spot, found one around the corner at the end of the block and carefully led Kate to it.

"Why won't you marry me?" he asked, when they were finally alone and he held her close.

"Can't marry you," she corrected. Her chest rose and fell against his as she took a deep breath. "Because you have no plans, no goals. No dreams. You think that riding bulls, even though it could kill you, is all you need."

"Wrong," he told her. When she looked up at him, his resolve to convince her that they belonged together forever grew stronger. "I don't ride bulls anymore. I'm officially retired from that."

Her eyes widened and brightened. "You are?"

Nodding, he smiled. "Anything else?"

The light in her eyes dimmed. "But why? You love rodeo."

"I realized I liked freckle-faced redheads much better than ornery bulls." He kissed the tip of her nose, then leaned back to look at her and saw something in her eyes he couldn't quite read. "There's something else, isn't there?"

Hesitating, she lowered her head. "No."

He placed a finger under her chin and tipped her face up, forcing her to look at him. "What is it, Kate? Tell me."

"I— It's just that I can't."

He felt a strange foreboding when she dipped her head again. "You can't what? Tell me? Marry me? We just went over the bull riding and rodeo."

"I don't want you giving it up for me."

"I'm not," he said. "I'm giving it up for me. It isn't what I want anymore. I want you."

She raised her head to meet his gaze. "Then you are giving it up for me. But that isn't the problem," she hurried on to say before he could tell he she was wrong. "I thought it was the bull riding, but it isn't. I'm still afraid."

"Of what?"

She took a deep breath before answering. "Of losing you. I lost my parents, the two people I loved the most. I can't lose you, too."

In that moment, he knew she loved him. "I was afraid, too," he admitted.

"Of what?" she asked.

"You were right, Kate. Risking my life would be wrong. You made me realize that. But I thought there wasn't a reason not to risk it. I thought there wasn't anybody who would be affected by what I did. You showed me there was."

"But—"

"And I was afraid of losing you. Of losing the life I want with you."

She shook her head. "You still don't have any plans for your future."

"Wrong again. I have lots of plans, and they all include you."

"Like what?"

"Like maybe merging our farms. If Aggie is agreeable, that is. Even if farming doesn't pay off, if that's
what's important to you, then it is to me, too. And I don't
care if you never boil as much as a pan of water or if
you turn a can of tuna into roast beef, I still want to
marry you."

She looked up at him, her blue eyes darkened with a
passion he'd never forget. "But what will you do?"

With a grin, he rocked her in his arms. "Well, there's
the rodeo stock company Tanner and I are starting up."
Her look of surprise pulled a chuckle from him. "And
we have someone special in mind to do our accounting." He pulled her closer, loving the feel of her. "And
when we're not working—and that will be a lot of the
time—I'll be busy loving you and filling the house
with babies." His voice dropped to a whisper. "If that's
what you want."

Kate's smile nearly knocked him over. She nodded.
"One at a time, though." Her smile dimmed, and her lips
drew down in a stubborn frown. "But we'll argue."

"And make up," he said, ducking his head to nibble
her neck. "And argue and make up, and— We'll never
be bored. And you'll never let me get a word in because
you'll be—"

"Dusty?"

He pulled back to look at her, wondering what else
she could think of to keep them apart. "What?"

"Just kiss me."

He barely noticed the cheers from the crowd that
had gathered again as he granted her request. She would

never be tamed, never be like anyone else, but that was one of the reasons why he loved her. She was all he would ever need.

* * * * *

*Look for Trish and Morgan's story this summer,
only from Roxann Delaney and
Harlequin American Romance!*

"AREN'T YOU GOING TO SAY 'Fly me' or at least 'Welcome
Aboard'?"

Amanda Bauer didn't. The softly muttered word that
actually came out of her mouth was a lot less welcoming. And had fewer letters. Four, to be exact.

The man shook his head and tsked. "Not exactly the
friendly skies. Haven't caught the spirit yet this morning?"

"Make one more airline-slogan crack and you'll be
walking to Chicago," she said.

He nodded once, then pushed his sunglasses onto
the top of his tousled hair. The move revealed blue eyes
that matched the sky above. And yeah. They were twinkling. Damn it.

"Understood. Just, uh, promise me you'll say 'Coffee,
tea or me' at least once, okay? Please?"

Amanda tried to glare, but that twinkle sucked the annoyance right out of her. She could only draw in a slow
breath as he climbed into the plane. As she watched her
passenger disappear into the small jet, she had to
wonder about the trip she was about to take.

Coffee and tea they had, and he was welcome to them.
But her? Well, she'd never even considered making a
move on a customer before. Talk about unprofessional.

And yet…

Something inside her suddenly wanted to take a
chance, to be a little outrageous.

How long since she had done indecent things—or decent ones, for that matter—with a sexy man? Not since before they'd thrown all their energies into expanding Clear-Blue Air, at the very least. She hadn't had time for a lunch date, much less the kind of lust-fest she'd enjoyed in her younger years. The kind that lasted for entire weekends and involved not leaving a bed except to grab the kind of sensuous food that could be smeared onto—and eaten off—someone else's hot, naked, sweat-tinged body.

She closed her eyes, her hand clenching tight on the railing. Her heart fluttered in her chest and she tried to make herself move. But she couldn't—not climbing up, but not backing away, either. Not physically, and not in her head.

Was she really considering this? God, she hadn't even looked at the stranger's left hand to make sure he was available. She had no idea if he was actually attracted to her or just an irrepressible flirt. Yet something inside was telling her to take a shot with this man.

It was crazy. Something she'd never considered. Yet right now, at this moment, she was definitely considering it. If he was available…could she do it? Seduce a stranger? Have an anonymous fling, like something out of a blue movie on late-night cable?

She didn't know. All she knew was that the flight to Chicago was a short one so she had to decide quickly. And as she put her foot on the bottom step and began to climb up, Amanda suddenly had to wonder if she was about to embark on the ride of her life.

"AREN'T YOU GOING to say 'Fly me' or at least 'Welcome aboard'?"

Amanda Bauer didn't. The softly muttered word that actually came out of her mouth was a lot less welcoming. And had fewer letters. Four, to be exact.

The man shook his head and tsked. "Not exactly the friendly skies. Haven't caught the spirit yet this morning?"

"Make one more airline-slogan crack and you'll be walking to Chicago," she said.

He nodded once, then pushed his sunglasses onto the top of his tousled hair. The move revealed blue eyes that matched the sky above. And yeah. They were twinkling. Damn it.

"Understood. Just, uh, promise me you'll say 'Coffee, tea or me' at least once, okay? Please?"

Amanda tried to glare, but that twinkle sucked the annoyance right out of her.

Coffee and tea they had, and he was welcome to them. But her? Well, she'd never even considered making a move on a customer before. Talk about unprofessional.

And yet...

Something inside her suddenly wanted to take a chance, to be a little outrageous.

How long since she had done indecent things—or

decent ones, for that matter—with a sexy man? She hadn't had time for a lunch date, much less the kind of lust-fest she'd enjoyed in her younger years. The kind that lasted for entire weekends and involved not leaving a bed except to grab the kind of sensuous food that could be smeared onto—and eaten off—someone else's hot, naked, sweat-tinged body.

She closed her eyes, her hand clenching tight on the railing. Her heart fluttered in her chest and she tried to make herself move.

Was she really considering this? She had no idea if he was actually attracted to her or just an irrepressible flirt. Yet something inside was telling her to take a shot with this man.

It was crazy. Something she'd never considered. Yet right now, at this moment, she was definitely considering it. If he was available...could she do it? Seduce a stranger. Have an anonymous fling, like something out of a blue movie on late-night cable?

She didn't know. All she knew was that the flight to Chicago was a short one, so she had to decide quickly. And as she put her foot on the bottom step and began to climb up, Amanda suddenly had to wonder if she was about to embark on the ride of her life.

Look for
PLAY WITH ME
by Leslie Kelly
Available February 2010

Silhouette Desire

Money can't buy him love…
but it can get his foot in the door

He needed a wife…fast. And Texan Jeff Brand's
lovely new assistant would do just fine. After all,
the heat between him and Holly Lombard was
becoming impossible to resist. And a no-strings
marriage would certainly work for them both—
but will he be able to keep his feelings out of
this in-name-only union?

Find out in

MARRYING
THE LONE STAR
MAVERICK

by *USA TODAY* bestselling author
SARA ORWIG

Available in February

Always Powerful, Passionate and Provocative!

SD73010

REQUEST YOUR FREE BOOKS!
2 FREE NOVELS PLUS 2 FREE GIFTS!

HARLEQUIN®

American Romance®

Love, Home & Happiness!

YES! Please send me 2 FREE Harlequin® American Romance® novels and my 2 FREE gifts (gifts are worth about $10). After receiving them, if I don't wish to receive any more books, I can return the shipping statement marked "cancel." If I don't cancel, I will receive 4 brand-new novels every month and be billed just $4.24 per book in the U.S. or $4.99 per book in Canada. That's a saving of close to 15% off the cover price! It's quite a bargain! Shipping and handling is just 50¢ per book in the U.S. and 75¢ per book in Canada.* I understand that accepting the 2 free books and gifts places me under no obligation to buy anything. I can always return a shipment and cancel at any time. Even if I never buy another book from Harlequin, the two free books and gifts are mine to keep forever.

154 HDN E4CC   354 HDN E4CN

Name _____ (PLEASE PRINT)

Address _____ Apt. #

City _____ State/Prov. _____ Zip/Postal Code

Signature (if under 18, a parent or guardian must sign)

Mail to the Harlequin Reader Service:
IN U.S.A.: P.O. Box 1867, Buffalo, NY 14240-1867
IN CANADA: P.O. Box 609, Fort Erie, Ontario L2A 5X3

Not valid for current subscribers to Harlequin® American Romance® books.

Want to try two free books from another line?
Call 1-800-873-8635 or visit www.morefreebooks.com.

* Terms and prices subject to change without notice. Prices do not include applicable taxes. N.Y. residents add applicable sales tax. Canadian residents will be charged applicable provincial taxes and GST. Offer not valid in Quebec. This offer is limited to one order per household. All orders subject to approval. Credit or debit balances in a customer's account(s) may be offset by any other outstanding balance owed by or to the customer. Please allow 4 to 6 weeks for delivery. Offer available while quantities last.

Your Privacy: Harlequin is committed to protecting your privacy. Our Privacy Policy is available online at www.eHarlequin.com or upon request from the Reader Service. From time to time we make our lists of customers available to reputable third parties who may have a product or service of interest to you. If you would prefer we not share your name and address, please check here. ☐

Help us get it right—We strive for accurate, respectful and relevant communications. To clarify or modify your communication preferences, visit us at www.ReaderService.com/consumerchoice.

HAR10